In the cosmopolitan coastal city of Adelaide in South Australia, two theater lovers create a little drama of their own . . .

Twenty-seven-year-old divorcée Vix Tremain finally has her first job—as a theater-set painter—and is ready to leave the past behind. What better way to get her confidence back than a fling with a handsome stranger? She isn't looking for anything emotional, she's had enough heartbreak. Rugged Jay Dee, the set construction manager, fits the bill for no strings fun perfectly.

What Vix doesn't realize is that Jay is not exactly a stranger . . .

Jay would recognize wealthy, spoiled Vix anywhere. After all, she's the ex-wife of the man who destroyed his career. Naturally, Jay wants a little sweet revenge—at first. To his surprise, Vix is far from the ice princess he expected, and spending time with her changes everything. Soon he realizes he's actually falling for the vulnerable beauty. But becoming entangled with her will mean revealing who he is—and opening them both up to more pain. With their dreams at stake, is their connection strong enough to weather the truth—and take center stage?

Books by Virginia Taylor

South Landers
Starling
Ella
Charlotte
Wenna

Romance By Design
Sets Appeal

Published by Kensington Publishing Corporation

Sets Appeal

A Romance By Design Novel

Virginia Taylor

LYRICAL PRESS
Kensington Publishing Corp.
www.kensingtonbooks.com

First Electronic Edition: April 2017
eISBN-13: 978-1-5161-0007-1
eISBN-10: 1-5161-0007-7

First Print Edition: April 2017
ISBN-13: 978-1-5161-0011-86
ISBN-10: 11-5161-0011-5

Printed in the United States of America

Acknowledgments

To my editor Marci Clark whose excellent judgment in picking Starling, my first published historical romance, gave me the chance to showcase my hometown in a series set in Adelaide, South Australia. Marci, you are the best editor in the whole world, bar none.

Chapter 1

Her shoulders almost creaking with tension, Victoria Tremain turned off her car engine. Tonight, as one of the crew, she had attended the first party she had been to in a year, a pre-production getting-to-know-you function held for the cast and crew of the stage version of *High Society*. Experiencing a deadly case of stage fright, she aimed the huge smile she had plastered on her face in the direction of her wildly attractive passenger. He had told her he would make her a cup of coffee if she drove him home.

Behind him, the blaring streetlight reflected on the outside of a suburban redbrick bungalow with no fence and a front garden that had been dug over but not planted—a work in progress, but not out of place in this narrow street of tidy post-war houses. Shadowy stacks of planks lay in his concrete driveway.

"So, this is where you build your theater sets?" Her voice sounded suitably low and husky, not because she was at all sophisticated, but because she was terrified.

Picking up men wasn't as easy as... Actually, she hadn't imagined picking up men would be easy, not for someone as naturally awkward as she. She had almost fallen over her feet in her hurry to get the hunky set-builder into her car. Or maybe she almost fell over her big yellow heels, which took some getting used to—for she was now flashy, single, champagne-drinking Vix Tremain, trying to find the life she had missed during the past seven years. Married at the age of twenty, she had divorced eleven months ago.

He shook his head. "The wood belongs in the garage, but I haven't had time yet to shift it." Muffled *doof-doof* music rocked the air as he opened the car door on his side.

She opened her side, stepped out, and caught her bag on the handbrake. Muttering under her breath, she untangled the strap and closed the door, hoping he hadn't noticed. His coordination was as notable as his big, honed body.

She cleared her throat. "When did you finish your last set?" Scooping her hair back, she followed him along an overgrown path to the low front porch.

"A couple of weeks ago. My team does four a year." He fumbled for his keys.

A sudden gust of wind blew a sheet of newspaper across the road and an orphaned takeaway coffee cup rattled against the fence. As she took a step back to give him space, her spiked heel caught between two slats and she stumbled.

He grabbed her, steadying her against his chest, his shaggy brown hair idly teasing across her cheek. "My woman trap." He set her back on her own feet. Suppressed laughter deepened his voice.

She gave a careful smile, scoring herself a ten for not apologizing. The man smelled like pine chips and the fresh sea breeze blowing in from the port. He opened the door, a forest green blistered over white undercoat and slivers of ashen wood. For a moment, his arm blocked her as he reached around his doorframe for the light. The pulse in her neck thudding, she waited until he stepped back. This could be her first one-night stand if she didn't mess up or say something dorky. Tonight, she had great expectations of herself. She had scrubbed-up quite well and now she only had to follow through.

He placed his hand on the center of her back and guided her through a bare hallway to an open space containing a sitting room at one end and a dining–slash–kitchen area at the other. Tossing his leather jacket over a chair, he stepped behind the kitchen countertop and began to pour coffee beans into a grinder sitting beside a basic espresso machine. For a moment, she experienced stark disappointment. Perhaps when he had said "coffee," he had meant "coffee."

"Take a seat." Using his eyes, he indicated the sitting area, painted in faded magnolia and furnished with a floral two-seater couch and a couple of stiff-backed chairs upholstered in gray.

Keeping him in view, she sat on the edge of the couch, clutching her handbag to her chest. Her mouth was as dry as the recent winter. "What's your real name?"

"JD." Resting his work-roughened hands on the countertop, he flitted his gaze over her legs.

Her skirt had hitched up too high. She thought about using her handbag as a cover but she had worn the bad-girl, tight red skirt to change her image.

Breathing out, she put the bag on the floor, giving him a sideways glance. "I'm guessing. An abbreviation of Juvenile Delinquent?" She held her breath.

He smiled, forming creases that were almost dimples. "From *West Side Story*?" He scooped the ground beans into the measure.

She half-relaxed. He recognized the musical, and most men didn't. "Just Deciding might suit you better." She laughed at her blatant hint but when his gaze connected with hers, her face warmed. He could take all the time he needed and if he didn't plan on having sex with her, the world wouldn't end. He might simply have wanted a comfortable ride home. Men invariably preferred using her cars.

Fortunately, he gave her an amused look. Reaching for the mugs, he showed her an impressive back view, wide at the top and angling to lean hips and a tight, hard rear. Although stacked, he couldn't be called handsome. The left side of his face had been puckered by a scar that wove up his cheek and toward his eye. He looked like the tradesman he was, an appearance he emphasized with his faded jeans and cotton shirt.

"How do you like your coffee?" He stared at her over his shoulder.

"Plain black, please."

At the party for *High Society*, she'd used champagne to segue into the new sophisticated Vix Tremain. Awkward, tactless Victoria Nolan had barely spoken to a man in this past year, let alone stumbled into his house. Married young, she'd never ventured into the dating scene. Instead, she had accepted the first man who had shown an interest in her, impressionable fool that she had been. "How complicated was your last set?"

"A single room." He shrugged. "Three entrances and a flight of stairs." He brought over a brimming coffee, placing the mug on the blue-painted table adjacent to her seat.

"Sit here," she said, amazing herself by patting the cushion beside her. She even considered adding a casual touch by kicking off her heels, but couldn't with any semblance of grace. Her legs were long and her skirt was a size tighter than she usually bought. She should have worn fitted pants. Then she could have crossed her legs or casually hooked one up onto the couch. Dressing to pick up a man needed more planning than she had imagined. She dragged in a breath. "I see we have ten scene changes. That's enough to keep me painting solidly for the next three months."

He lowered himself beside her. For a few heartbeats, he sat silently. "Are you being paid for your time or the job?"

"For the job. My specialty is set design, but I've never worked. I have to start. So, I thought taking on the painting first would ease my way in, which makes the money immaterial."

He gave an almost imperceptible nod. "When did it happen?"

"Getting the job?"

"I'm asking about your divorce." He lifted her third finger, left hand, which still held an indented reminder of the wedding ring she no longer wore.

She no longer owned the platinum band, either. Although she should have flushed the meaningless thing into the sewer, she couldn't stand waste. Instead, she had gone out to buy herself a box of celebration chocolates, the last she had eaten since then, and sold the ring, dropping the money into the hat of the first street musician she saw on the way back to her car. "You're observant. I've been free for a year."

"Good."

She tilted her head to the side, trying an unconcerned smile. "Because?"

His eyebrows lifted.

Her insides began to quiver with hope.

He settled his arm along the back of the couch. His hand touched her hair, and he tugged a lock. "What am I going to do with you?" He used a deep, soft tone.

"Did you have anything else in mind when you offered to make me coffee?" Her tentative gaze met his.

"Not my thinking mind, no."

"Your thinking mind as compared to...?"

He drew air through his teeth. "As compared to the mind I don't often use when I'm with a beautiful woman. So..." He rested one large hand on the side of her neck and his thumb under her jaw. Leaning over, he touched his lips to hers.

A delicious shiver ran though her. His eyelashes were thick and brown at the tips and blond near his lids.

When she could breathe evenly, she said, "You have nice, soft lips."

"That's my line." His steady gaze held hers.

"I thought you might need encouragement."

His mouth tilted at the corners and his eyes gleamed. "More likely discouragement."

She gave an off-hand shrug, smiling inside. "I'm just not in the mood to do that," she said, trying for a mock snooty tone.

"To discourage me?" He glanced sideways at her. "Let me get this straight. You want to encourage me?"

"I drove you home. What would you expect if you had driven me home?" She lifted her eyebrows.

He nodded. "I would hope for much more than a cup of coffee."

She couldn't look away from him, and she certainly couldn't breathe.

He meshed his fingers with hers. "And, fair's fair." Staring at her face, he put his other arm along the back of the couch behind her. His hand shifted to the nape of her neck and she found herself tucked into his frame.

She glanced up, hoping to be kissed again.

He obliged, dropping his mouth lightly over hers and testing her upper lip with his tongue.

She drew back. "The bedroom?"

"Right now?"

Experimentally, she brushed his upper thigh with her knuckles, noting an exciting shape expanding his jeans. "I can't possibly give you time to change your mind."

He picked up her hand and gently took the pad of her forefinger between his lips. "Why hurry? We're going to be working together," he said in a relaxed voice.

"Not often. When your job ends, mine begins. I can't paint a set before it's built."

He toyed with her fingers.

She wriggled uncomfortably. "If you're afraid of awkwardness when we meet again, I'm sure we will hardly ever meet again. I mean…"

"So, you want to get into bed with someone that you expect to hardly ever meet again?"

Her insides began to shake. "If you don't want to, you can say no. I thought… Well, it's kind of normal, isn't it, to have an instant physical attraction to someone? Well, it's not normal for me, but…"

He leaned back, staring into her eyes. "I didn't plan on saying no."

"Are we arguing about what happens next, or are we agreeing?" She started to chew on her lip and, mindful of looking insecure, stopped.

He glanced away. "What color are my eyes?"

"You have light brown hair, so you probably have light eyes."

"Your eyes are blue."

"You're looking straight at them now," she said indignantly.

"How does that follow? You're not naturally blond."

"I almost am."

He laughed.

Embarrassed, for she had been born blond and had remained that way until about the age of ten, when her hair had turned a pure shade of natural mouse, she said, "Hardly anyone is at my age. If you are only interested in natural blondes, you're doomed to disappointment."

"I didn't say I was disappointed. My mind was simply trying to connect eye color and hair color."

"I can only judge your reaction to me by your, um..." She stopped, knowing she shouldn't tell a man that from the moment they'd met, his smile had lured her on, way past her normal comfort zone. Most men preferred assured women who knew how to tease.

"My *um?*" His expression blanked, and he stood.

Her stomach dropped to her toes. Being knocked back on her first try at propositioning a man would probably put her off ever trying again. Any other unnatural blonde in a tight red skirt would get the man she wanted... or leave with her dignity intact. She rose to her feet, avoiding his eyes. "So, I'll say goodnight and thank you for the coffee."

He stood. "You read my *um* right. That's one of the disadvantages of being male."

She nodded, reaching for her handbag. A tall, confident man like him was possibly propositioned twice a day, at least. He could afford to pick and choose. Her breath stopped as she realized what he had implied and, her mouth not quite shut, she lifted her gaze to his.

"And thank me in the morning," he murmured as his mouth slowly connected with hers.

At first stunned, she didn't respond. Then he settled a palm on the small of her back, drawing her close. Her insides began to hum, and she leaned away to struggle out of her jacket. He helped, tossing the distraction onto the chair with his. She started to work on the button of his jeans, her brain a maze of unfinished thoughts. Unfortunately, in her confusion, she tangled her fingers against his flat belly.

"I'll do that," he said, his eyes glinting with humor. "I think I ought to head for the bathroom for a condom. The bedroom is through there." He indicated the room in the hallway closest to the front door.

She glanced at his chin, traced her gaze over his scar, and straightened her shoulders. Then, picking up her jacket and her bag, she went into his bedroom, where after undressing quickly, she arranged herself in his bed. With her arms at her sides, she lay staring at the flaky ceiling, forcing in long, deep breaths. He gave her time enough to ease the nervous flutter in her chest and time enough to justify acting out of character.

She had never before let anyone think they owed her a favor. A good girl all her life, she had been called prissy and conventional. She'd watched the bad girls grab whatever they wanted while she'd stood back and hoped to be valued for being honest. No more.

She'd been cheated on, taken advantage of, and left humiliated. If she had any sort of courage, she would stop living for tomorrow and start living for today—tonight. What sort of person had no regrets? Wincing, she glanced at her clothes on the floor. If need be she could make a quick getaway.

In half an hour, with luck, she would find out if sex with a wildly attractive bad boy would change her attitude. She didn't care about competing with other more attractive, more confident women, and she didn't hope for love. One single bout of satisfying sex would do her. Then, she would know she was not as frigid, repressed, and sexless as she had been told.

Staring at the door, she waited for the big, inscrutable hunk.

* * * *

Jay shut the bathroom door behind him. Last year, he had built the set for *South Pacific*. Although he hadn't attended any rehearsals of the show, while he had been bumping-in the set, he had heard an actor going over a schmaltzy song about spotting a woman across a crowded room and falling instantly in love.

Jay hadn't fallen instantly in love with Vix Tremain, but lust had featured strongly. Spotting the blonde, he had pushed through the usual crowd to introduce himself to a sleek beauty who seemed genuinely glad to talk him. Normally a woman with skin as smooth as rich cream and a long-legged, toned body would act like a show pony, but she had a rare natural charm. She also showed a clear interest in him, demonstrated by the odd self-conscious gesture, like touching her hair and moistening her lips. Every move of hers reflected his purely animal attraction. He'd thought the last theater set he ever meant to construct would easily be his most interesting.

Set painters could be anyone—male or female, old or young, ultra-serious, control freaks, or dreadlocked posers. Not often did he get assigned to a beautiful woman who looked as interested in messing around as he was. He didn't have the time for a relationship, but he could fit in a casual affair that lasted the length of the production, and he could certainly handle one with a golden man-toy. He'd been blatant about his attraction to her, and he'd intimated that a sweaty night would be had by all if she accompanied him home.

The dazzling smile she gave him in response hit him like a punch to the head. He'd seen that smile before. Only last year, when skimming the newspaper, he'd noted a photograph of the Nolans, plain, plump Victoria with her incredible smile and her older husband, Timothy, architect and millionaire entrepreneur.

Jay ran his fingers over the scar on his cheek, a memento from her husband.

For at least a year, he'd thought about revenge on Timmy-boy. Although Jay was visibly scarred, he'd never been handsome. Nor did he make his living out of his looks. Bygones had been bygones, but knowing she was

Tim's ex added to her appeal. In fact, he'd seen screwing her as some sort of compensation for having his future screwed by Tim. His dick had largely guided these self-serving thoughts.

Now, although still influenced by a keen body part, he found he couldn't use Vix in an act of silent revenge. Perhaps if she had been the woman he'd always assumed she was, a rich bitch with haughty opinions, he wouldn't have changed sides, but a sophisticated man-toy she was not. Instead, she was bright and wryly funny, both of which he found more sexually stimulating than a bored divorcée looking for a night on the wild side.

Crap! He couldn't knock back a woman with so little confidence in herself. If he had her, he would be all kinds of a heel. If he didn't, he would be all kinds of a fool.

He massaged the back of his neck, undecided.

Finally, he eked out a breath, opened the cabinet door, and glumly reached for a condom. This had to be his unluckiest night in his whole misbegotten life.

Chapter 2

Vix tried to ease her shoulders. Not knowing which was JD's preferred side of the bed, she had taken the middle, lying on her back, hands at her side, looking available—or looking like a tomb effigy. Sighing, she sat up, chin on her knees, fingers thrumming on her shins. Perhaps posing on her side, one hand under her head and facing the door would look more appealing, more casual. She quickly rolled, wishing she had something to do while she waited, but a woman couldn't do a lot in a strange bedroom other than wait and try not to feel apprehensive.

Finally, the bathroom door opened and he appeared in the bedroom doorway, still dressed. He tilted his eyebrows at her, stalked toward her, and dropped a single packaged condom onto the bedside table nearest the door. Taking the hint, she scooted to the other side, staring at him. He stared back, his eyes refocusing on her lacy, flesh-colored underwear. With a sexy hitch of his mouth, he pulled his shirt over his head, baring a lightly fuzzed upper body packed with muscles. Her breath shortened.

She didn't want to stare, but he had a physique nothing short of magnificent. Turning his back on her, he sat on the bed and removed his shoes. He stood to unbutton his waistband, but before unzipping, he picked up his socks, shoes, and shirt. In a bundle, he tossed everything into his wardrobe and, as she watched, his jeans followed.

He looked stunning from the back view. Surely, a rough-around-the-edges man like him would get her through this. Unfortunately, she could barely breathe after he turned. The well-marked length of his enormous erection showed clearly beneath his cotton jocks. She moistened her dry mouth, holding the bed cover so tightly that her fingers locked. As he swung onto the bed beside her, she swooped the covering to her chin in an automatic reaction.

"Shouldn't you be naked?" He sounded relaxed.

She cleared her throat, willing herself not to blush. "Shouldn't you?"

"Not yet." Facing her, the expression on his face looked wary. He ran a thumb slowly across her collarbone.

She shivered, a reaction she couldn't control. "Could you turn out the light?"

"I could. Do I have to?"

"Yes." She swallowed.

He swiveled around and switched off the bedside lamp. The heat of his body hovered, and she could smell toothpaste, which she now wished she had used. As her eyes grew accustomed to the dark, she could see his looming shape as he gathered her up against him. His overlong silky hair touched her cheek, tickling, and his bristles scraped her chin. Then, his palm slipped beneath the strap of her bra. She put up a hand to stop him, but he snapped the elastic onto her upper arm.

Reacting like a petulant schoolgirl, she pushed against his hard shoulders. "No, don't."

"Don't what?" His mouth slid from her chin to the top of her breast.

"Don't touch me. Just do what you have to."

"Okay," he said, his tone careful. Within a second, he was sitting on her thighs.

She wouldn't have minded lying that way forever, or at least until she could regulate her breathing, but she assumed she would eventually have to move her legs. Fortunately, he couldn't see her or the expression on her face, which would be somewhere between nervous and puzzled. She tried to sound interested in proceeding. "Are you going to keep sitting on me?" she said in what she hoped sounded like a sophisticated voice. Her heart thudded like a drum.

"If I did, that would make doing what I have to do fairly difficult." He pushed her hair back with a single, casual finger, a gentle touch like a caress, but he didn't need to placate her. He simply needed to get the whole thing over and done with. "What's your next order?"

"I don't have one." She wet her lips.

"Well, do you mind if I follow my own plan?"

"As long as... No, please go ahead," she said, at a loss and wishing she didn't want to tear the sheet off his bed and run. She hadn't thought the whole encounter through. A man like him, well, he would be ultra-experienced. Women would flock around him. He would need to bat them off. She had chosen wisely, but she didn't have the nous to follow through. Breathing through her nose, she tried to relax.

He took each of her hands in his and, calloused palm against stiff palm, he raised them to the pillow beside her head. His mouth touched on hers, and stayed, lightly teasing. Her breathing sped up, her skin heated, and she tingled where she should. Now would be a good time to get the act over and done with. She arched her back, prepared to change to a more promising position while he buried his face into her neck, his breath shorter than she might have expected. Then, his knees edged hers apart. She tensed as his shape pressed between her legs. He exhaled and his grip froze.

Momentarily, she coped with the heightening sensation but he made a noise like a growl and slid down farther down her body, taking both her bra straps to her elbows. She flipped her chest sideways. "No. Please."

He rolled off her, sat up, and turned on the light, blinking at her. With a wary expression on his face, he said, "How about a glass of milk?"

"A glass of milk? You don't want to…you can't…I didn't mean…I just don't like being naked."

"So you implied." He eased off the bed and disappeared.

She sat hugging herself, hearing him clatter in the kitchen. She should leave. At the very least, she should be fully dressed when he returned, not foolishly expecting him to try again. Her eyes heated, and she blinked hard. Although he'd implied he would be cooperative, apparently if he couldn't do as he wished, he wouldn't do anything, and what he wanted to do was paw her all over.

Her chin at an upward tilt, she moved to the side of the bed. If he preferred being in the kitchen to having sex with a willing woman, he could swill to his heart's content. Then again, her pride wouldn't let her escape until she had made a concerted effort. Chewing at her forefinger, she slid her cold feet back under the spread. While she made no decision whatsoever, he reappeared holding two frosted glasses. He placed one on the console beside her.

"Do you not like being touched by me, or by anyone?"

She reached for the milk. "I think touching is unnecessary, that's all. It puts me off when I'm prepared to…when I'm willing to…when I'm thinking about…oh, great heavens, I don't find these things easy to talk about." She cleared her throat and took a sip of her drink. "And you're my first anyone, aside from my husband—my ex."

He bent his head and gazed into his glass. "Your first, huh? That's a flattering disadvantage. I don't know what I'm competing with here, but

I imagine every man has his own way of doing things. I like to take my time and play around for a while before sex."

"I like to get the act over with."

He gave her a sidelong glance while he slowly rubbed his bristled jaw. Then he shrugged. "I like women. I like to touch. I know what pleasures me. I like to see my woman pleasured, too. If I have to forgo that, I might as well jerk myself off."

She straightened, grimacing. "Crudely put, but basically if I don't let you touch me, I don't get anything?"

"Right," he said in a confident drawl. "You get the full trip or nothing at all."

"This isn't fair."

His eyebrows lifted as if he was waiting for her to change her mind.

For a moment, she wavered. "Then, you'll get what you want, but I won't." Hoping she sounded logical rather than petulant, she leaned back.

"I'm willing to go without if I can't have what I want. Are you?" He pulled at his earlobe.

"There's a difference," she said, her voice husky with embarrassment. She cleared her throat. "I don't know what I want." Resting her cheek on her up-drawn knees, she angled her head away from him.

The black of night showed through the white roller blind. No window in his house had been curtained. His floors were bare wood and not a single wall held a picture. He owned nothing but the bare essentials and none looked new or trendy. She had assumed he owned this house when she'd entered, but likely he didn't. This was a rental, and he'd recently moved in.

"You want me," he said in a secure voice. "But…I'm more than my dick."

She reached over him and carefully placed her empty glass on his bedside table. "And what else do you think made me come here with you?"

"You drove me here."

"For one reason. And you haven't even opened the condom." Her bottom lip quivered, and she felt as unattractive as a woman could be.

"I'm not ready."

"You look ready."

"Peeking, are you? Well, then, perhaps I ought to open the condom." With a frown of concentration, he reached for the plastic pack that he didn't seem able to open. He tried tearing across one corner and then the other. He tried with his teeth. He sighed. "Damn."

"Haven't you done this before?"

He didn't answer.

"Pass it to me." She reached over him.

He evaded her. The pack ripped in two in his hands. Unfortunately, the condom ripped, too. He sat with a ring in one hand and a bubble in the other. He slowly turned his head, and he stared her straight in the eyes. "Now what?"

"Don't you have another?"

"What do you think?"

"Surely you buy these things in multiples." She frowned.

"Sure, if I am expecting to use them in multiples. I didn't know you'd insist on me dropping my pants on the first date."

"This isn't a date."

He lifted his palms. "So, you've answered your own question. I suppose I could go out and buy some, but I don't have a car. You would have to drive me."

"I might as well go home if I have to dress and leave." She glanced at his semi-naked, beautiful body, and her insides curled with frustration. "Perhaps this was meant to be."

He put the remains of the condom on the table. "The hand of man moves in mysterious ways." He gave a soft laugh. "At least this takes the pressure off. We don't have to do anything we don't want to do."

"Don't have to?" she echoed hollowly. Her feet found his cold floorboards again, this time more decisively. "I'll go." She reached for her skirt, determined not to look at him again.

"This is great," he said in a morose voice. "JD. Just Dick."

"Look, I came here for sex. I don't want another glass of milk. We don't know each other well enough to have a deep and meaningful convers—"

He tipped her onto the bed. "We can rectify that."

She stared into his strong-boned face, and he dropped a wonky kiss on the side of her mouth. One muscled arm lifted her and gathered her against his warm chest.

"We can do quite a bit of getting to know each other, or if you won't let me touch you, you can do quite a bit of getting to know me. By touch."

"And why would I want to do that?" Her insides began to jitter. From the very first, he had put a smile on her face and a hot tickle in her belly. He made her hope, and she couldn't remember the last time she had hoped for anything. Mainly, she had endured, and she had expected to endure forever, because she was, after all, a Tremain, a member of a family known for sheer hard work since the days of colonial settlement.

His warm breath heated her ear. "Because I feel good."

And because he did, she slid both palms over his back, noting that he flexed each muscle she touched. His confidence and his encouragement helped. To have half a sensuous experience doubled that she'd had previously.

"What do you do when you're not building sets?" she said against his hard, warm chest, palms resting lightly on his smooth skin.

"Any sort of construction." He switched off the bedside lamp.

She lifted herself onto one forearm. "I'm supposed to be touching you."

"Yeah, well, too much touching, and we won't get any sleep."

He pulled up the cover, circling an arm around the small of her back. She relaxed into him, resting her head on his shoulder, her hand comfortable on his bicep. He was warm and calm, and he breathed slowly and deeply. When he fell asleep, she could have left. But she felt safe.

And she, too, slept.

* * * *

"Hey, JD!"

Jay moved his face out of the pillow and opened his eyes.

"How was last night?" called the same female voice that wasn't coming from the startled blonde nestled against his chest.

"You have a visitor," Vix said in a whisper, looking panicked.

Curling his hand over her hip, he kissed the tip of her nose. She looked as lovely in the morning as she had the night before, and he wanted her as much as he had the night before. Maybe he could…

The fridge door slammed. "Champagne. Can I open it?" he heard from the kitchen.

He lifted himself on one elbow, focused, frowned, and rolled over to face the door. "No," he shouted as he sat up and leaped out of the bed in two quick motions. "Shit."

"Don't be pathetic," Ilona yelled. "You bought it for me. I'll bring in two glasses."

"No!" He pulled on his jeans. "I'll come out there." He sped out of the bedroom, in full grump mode, arriving in the kitchen in time to see Ilona slide a bottle of champagne onto the table. "Put that back."

She gave him a sideways, flirtatious smile and found two clean champagne glasses. "You dressed just for me?"

"Give me a break."

"Normally you sleep naked." With an uncaring expression on her face, she finger-combed her long blond hair, arranging the bulk over one shoulder and giving her seductive pout.

"What do you want?"

She wore panda eye makeup and her short tight skirt looked like a bandana, missing only the knot. "Something to eat. Were you saving that pizza for anyone?"

"Couldn't you simply raid the fridge and leave me to sleep?" He put the champagne back in the fridge but took out last night's leftover pizza and placed it on the table for her.

"Don't be a grouch. Give me a cuddle." She walked into his arms where she stayed, rubbing her face against his bare chest. "Mm-mm. I love you, Jay. You've got the tightest behind in the world." She groped the aforesaid, which annoyed the hell out of him, but remaining patient, he put her hand behind her. She laughed softly.

"Take the pizza and go." He kissed her forehead, messed her hair, and moved out of her reach.

"Where did you get the car? Did you rob a bank?" She picked up the slice of pizza and took a bite. Her expression looked too casual.

He blinked, remembering Vix's Mercedes outside. His shoulders stiffened. "It belongs to a friend."

"Who?" She glanced towards the bedroom.

He suppressed the urge to guard the door. If these two women ever met, the last place should be in his bedroom. Knowing women, he would be the one attacked for a situation not of his making. "No one you know. What's the time?"

"About eight. I'm on my way home. Late night. I thought I'd stop by and tell you I won't be going today. You don't mind, do you?" She took another big bite of the pizza.

"No. That's okay."

Her focus again on the bedroom, she nodded. "See you later, then. Thanks for the breakfast." She snatched up the remains of the pizza slice and, with her high heels clattering across the floorboards, she left by the back door for which she had a key.

One day he would ask for his key back, but he couldn't abandon her yet. She needed him, if only for champagne and pizza breakfasts, and while she was free to drop by whenever she chose, he knew she was okay.

Now he had to make his explanations in the bedroom, which he approached cautiously, wondering why. He'd slept with Vix, yes, but that was all. The crisp underwear she'd arrived in had barely been disturbed, unfortunately. He found, despite his body having other ideas, that he couldn't casually screw a woman who was afraid of sex. This said nothing for her ex-husband. Nor did her lack of confidence, which he'd spent his waking time last night trying not to erode further, and he also wondered why.

"Keep looking," he said, cheered by the way her big blue eyes skimmed over him as he walked through the doorway of the bedroom. "I don't mind being admired."

"So who admires you?"

"Too bad about that condom."

"Too bad about your mother."

"Who?"

"No doubt that was your mother in the kitchen?" She gave him a faked smile.

"Nope." He moved towards her, knowing she'd been married to an unfaithful prick who clearly hadn't treated her well in the bedroom. Jay was a sucker for a woman in distress. Vix also had body issues, which she hadn't changed by making her figure into one of the shapeliest he had ever seen. Although her most noticeable attributes were physical, in all the subjects they had covered at the party while tentatively assessing each other as bedmates, not once had she talked about herself.

He knew her opinion on the weather, musicals versus plays, comedies versus tragedies, the last musical to hit town, the university drama course, and the benefits of volunteering to get a job. And nothing about herself, other than hearsay from Ilona, in that she hadn't deserved her rich, brilliant husband, Tim Nolan.

As she had last night, she pulled the covers to her chin. Her hair looked messy but glossed with health, and her eyes shone with suspicion. "Are you going to tell me who she is?"

He stared at her, contemplating a morning of exploratory sex now that they knew more about each other. A one-night stand with her would have been doomed to fail. She thought she wanted a hard dick and nothing more. Apparently, that was all she'd ever had. He could give her much more. He could give her pleasure. If he had taken her last night, she would have been shocked by his speed, and so would he. A quick screw wasn't for him, nor for a woman who needed much more, though at this stage, he didn't quite know what she needed. He only knew he didn't perform to order, though of course he could have. The moment he had seen her, he had wanted her but he wanted her to relax and enjoy sex the way he did. He wanted her to enjoy him.

"I'll have the first shower," he said, breathing through his teeth. He was the master of self-punishment. "She's just a friend, no one you need worry about."

"Nothing worries me," said the woman who was afraid of him looking at her naked body in the light. "I just wanted to be sure that I'm not the wrong part of a threesome."

He gave her a light kiss on the lips and went to his wardrobe, snatching out a few articles of clothing. She had been the wrong part of a threesome while she was married. Lonny, the other participant, had just walked out his door.

During the next couple of months, if his attraction to this surprisingly appealing woman didn't fade, his balancing act would be a tad shaky.

* * * *

With a smile on her face, Vix stepped into JD's slippery bath to take a shower. JD was clearly attracted to her, which was pretty darned fantastic, but he and she weren't meant to be. The condom had proved that. He'd made her feel sexy, but nothing had happened. She could leave this morning without any regrets and without feeling cheap. And never, ever, would she drink too much again.

She wondered how his face had looked before the scar. Probably not quite as tough. He had regular features with a good strong nose and jaw. His skin was clear and tanned and his stubble held a glint of gold. The old white line of his scar was only a slight disfiguration. Before he'd asked, she hadn't concentrated on his eye color, just the appealing gleam of interest, but after he had questioned her, she had noted the unusual khaki green.

She washed her hair with his man-shampoo, knowing that with squeaky-clean hair she wouldn't feel so bad about not putting on fresh underwear. Maybe she could send him a big box of chocolates to thank him for his consideration last night. She would mention the doubtful state of her sobriety, which would excuse her slutty behavior. Though, his tousled, bristled look this morning was still a turn on. She blew out a breath, awed by the over-activity of her hormones.

After rinsing off, she stepped out of the bath and wrapped herself in a thin blue towel. Looking for a hair dryer, she searched his bathroom cabinet, but she didn't find one. However, she did find a box of condoms big enough to give the impression he could service the whole of the state's sexually active females without having to buy extra supplies.

She sucked in her bottom lip, even more ashamed of herself. The woman in the kitchen this morning must have been his girlfriend. For some reason, she hadn't attended the production party with him last night and today she had cancelled a date. He hadn't taken this amiss. Clearly, he and she trusted each other, and with good reason. Last night, he had faked the condom mishap with Vix because he didn't know how else to get himself off the hook with a prospective workmate who had practically ordered him to service her, as if she had the right.

Her face flared red and hot. Champagne was clearly far more insidious than she thought. She tried to remember if he had been drinking, but although he had filled her glass, he hadn't been holding one of his own.

However, despite not being even slightly intoxicated, he had wanted her. Even someone inexperienced with men could see that. At the party, his gaze had lingered on her face and his eyes had gleamed with interest. Without a hint from her, he suggested the ride home, and when he said coffee, his voice had purred with innuendo. In bed, his physical reaction was blatant and quite exciting. Although she didn't know too much about men, she knew an aroused male when she saw one. Given the opportunity to be unfaithful...he couldn't, unlike her ex-husband.

She toweled her hair as dry as she could and dressed quickly. Preparing to be as casual about the awkward morning-after as he was, she re-entered the bedroom, gathered up her handbag, retraced her steps to the bathroom, and applied her makeup. Without a hair dryer, her hair behaved unfashionably. Sighing, she swirled a knot on the top of her head and, holding the bun in place, she padded into the kitchen, knowing her blond hair looked fake and her skirt was too short and tight.

He stood over an ancient electric stove, which over the years had been chipped of white enamel on the corners, watching a pan full of sizzling calories. He smiled at her.

Her hormones overreacted with a perceptible thud. "Do you have a pencil I can borrow?" she asked in a voice that came out husky. She evaded his gaze.

He reached into an overhead cupboard and pulled one out. "Will this do?"

She wriggled the HB through her hair. "I hope you're not cooking break—"

"You look nice."

She angled her head on the side. "You don't need to fake interest."

"Okay. I'll file that. How many eggs do you want?"

"One."

"Should I flip over your egg?"

"No. Oh, glory. I haven't had a fried egg in a year." She sat at the gray-painted table that matched the gray-painted chairs that screamed to be stripped along with the lovely, uncovered Baltic pine floor.

"I hope you're not allergic."

"Only to calories." She cleared her throat. If she tried for a normal conversation, she could get through this awkwardness. "They're gorgeous old chairs, those clunky ones. I suspect you would find satinwood beneath that gray paint. They're art deco, I think."

"Like this table and the chairs. They all starred in *Noel and Gertie* and they've been heavily repaired by me, which is how I got them as a job lot for forty dollars after the production."

"*Noel and Gertie*? I saw that."

"What did you think?"

"The set was shades of gray, although only four, and Noel and Gertie wore black and white throughout the show. The old film look was effective, and I would have been impressed if I hadn't known it was a copy of the Broadway set."

"Did you see the Broadway show?"

She nodded. "Before I was married, when I wanted to see every set I could."

"I didn't know it was a copy." He rubbed his chin. "I built that set from... er, the designer's drawings."

"You don't have to name names. He always copies his sets. It's a shame there's no copyright. I don't understand people who don't want to experiment with ideas of their own."

"Nor do I. Speaking of which, you heard me stood up this morning. I don't need a date, but you might be interested in coming, anyway."

She lifted her eyebrows. "Because?"

"We'll be in the warehouse we use for set-building. It's where you'll be painting, too. You might want to look the place over while we're playing indoor volleyball."

"Who is *we*?"

"The construction team. We like to keep fit."

"So do I. How did you plan to get there?"

"My date would have driven me." With wide-eyed mock innocence, he pressed his lips together and leaned back, watching her face, having finished at least half his full plate of bacon and eggs.

Trying not to smile, she gave him a cool, so-that's-why-you-want-me glance, which she wished she had given to Tim. "Do you only ask women who own cars to be your dates?"

"It's cheaper than getting taxis." He lowered his chin and gazed at her. And he gave her that creased, almost dimpled, smile again.

She laughed. If she checked the paints and brushes today, she would know what she needed tomorrow when she planned to buy her supplies.

Since nothing had happened last night, she could put aside the episode. Today she and JD could be the workmates they should be. Probably.

Chapter 3

Rustic and picturesque, the massive old corrugated iron shed was sited in one of the small streets on the perimeter of the city of Adelaide. Because of Vix's insistence on stopping at her own house to change her clothes, and consequently being late, Jay gave a regal wave through the car's window to the construction team, who sat propped against a wall rusty with copper streaks.

For twenty minutes, he had sprawled in her car, which she had driven to Walkerville, a small, exclusive suburb between his not-so-classy suburb, Port Adelaide, and the city. After she had parked on a street with wide green verges and big shady street trees, she had disappeared behind the brushwood fence that hid her house. His wait was not unrewarded. She looked as delicious in her tight designer jeans and yellow loafers as she did in her red suit last night, though perhaps a little less self-conscious.

She pulled up her luxurious Mercedes sedan in the designated car park, surfaced with cracked concrete and plastered with dried mud from the rain last week.

"Was your girlfriend going to play volleyball?" she asked after a quick glance at the four-man, three-woman team, who needed Jay's key to get inside the building.

"Careful. Too much more questioning and I'll suspect you want more than a one condom fling." Seeing he had embarrassed her, he relented. "Lonny's not my girlfriend. She and I have known each other since we were five."

"And she is also part of your construction team?"

"No. I just take her out when she has nothing else to do." The waiting look on her face wanted him to continue, but he didn't have anything else to say.

She opened her door after a wry little twist of her lips. "I'll look at the paint supplies first. The production budget is generous and I can buy whatever I need, but I don't know what I need until I see what's here."

He nodded, opened his door, and stepped out. The guys had casual, noncommittal expressions on their faces, which meant they would put him through a bit of hard-line questioning about Vix.

"This is Vix, guys," he said, hoping he could preempt a grilling as he strode past everyone to the door. He shoved the key in the lock. "She's the set painter."

"Hi, Vix," Sherry, his brother Luke's wife, said, trying not to look too interested. "I'll introduce you to everyone, since JD seems to have forgotten our names."

"She met Trent and Steve last night." Jay leaned on the double-height door, which creaked open. The space inside was light-filled, courtesy of a large, dusty glass panel in the roof. Sparkling motes floated from there to the floor. The flats and cutouts of old sets covered the walls, some hung high, most left around for recycling.

"Of course," Vix said, apparently recognizing the two grinning guys he'd been with before she'd arrived at the party and been whisked away by Jay. "I didn't realize you were set builders, too."

"And this is Luke, my man and JD's brother." Sherry wrinkled her little snub nose at Jay. She was pretty, dark haired, and dark eyed, a contrast to Luke, who was stocky, red haired, and freckled. "So is Kellen, who brought two dates today, in case JD needed one. Lonny doesn't always turn up."

Jay's middle brother, Kellen, dark and dangerous, had a groupie addiction and chose his girls in batches, though how he decided which one he would keep for the night Jay never quite understood. Perhaps The Killer kept both. They looked the same, willing and able, with long straight hair, and he might not realize he had two instead of one. Jay nodded and smiled generally, trying to not look possessive of classy Vix, while he suppressed the urge to smack the calculation off Steve's and Trent's faces.

Dropping a guiding hand onto her hip, he turned her in the direction of the shed within a shed, where the paint supplies were kept by the company who owned the warehouse and employed Jay to make various sets for various stage shows. "You can look over your stuff away from these prying eyes."

For a moment, she watched Steve and Trent as they found the posts for the net. "How many do you have on a volleyball team?"

"Two, minimum, but it depends on how many turn up to play."

A couple of years ago, he had needed to use the volleyball game to warm up and relax the guys. These days, now expecting work from them, he used the volleyball game for mere enjoyment. After the game finished, they would pull apart old flats and reclaim whatever wood or composite sheeting was reclaimable. Most of the backing lengths had been used three or four times. With his job pricing, the lower the costs, the higher the wages.

He opened the paint-room door and steered Vix inside a space stacked with cans, dirty, paint-dried brushes, old tins, a plastic bucket, empty ice cream containers, rope, and a broken chair. "Sorry about the mess."

She lifted a can from on top of an unsettling pile of four. "Someone seems to have been trying to save money. This is house paint, probably found in the cheap bins, and the colors have been premixed." If a nose could curl, hers did. "They're no use other than to the painter who bought them."

"Put them in a pile and I'll get rid of them. I'll leave you to it." Determined to keep his working relationship with her professional, he went to help tie the net to the poles.

"Lonny always said you were a cocksman," Steve said in an undertone, shifting a couple of flats to make more room for the game. A little shorter than Jay, he was solid muscle. Every month or so, he added another tattoo to his sleeves of ink. "I'm beginning to believe it."

"She never said you were." Trent, tall and bony, with his fair hair shaved at the sides, punched the face of the grinning woman inked onto Steve's tricep.

Steve considered his reply. "She said you didn't have one."

Jay sighed. "Give it a rest."

Both men, part of his old gang from school days, had left dead-end construction work to help him start his set-building business, and from there, they'd moved ahead in leaps and bounds. Each had branched out into more specialized building jobs, Trent recently qualifying as a bricklayer and Steve as a plasterer, but both rejoined him as extra labor whenever he needed them.

Luke, his youngest brother, normally a plumber, helped out when his employers went into recess over summer, needing steady money to support his ever-growing family. At the age of twenty-six, he had three kids and had only started being responsible after the birth of the first. Kellen, Jay's uneven-tempered middle brother, was a cabinetmaker.

And neither Jay, nor Kellen, nor Luke, had ever had sex with Ilona, the first two being too young for her, and Jay more interested in being a protector than a predator, unlike every other guy who had taken advantage of Ilona's need to prove how attractive she was.

"Did you order the wood for the frames?" Steve kicked a few short lengths out of the way.

"What do you think?"

"So, it'll be full-on tomorrow?"

"The show will be bumped-in in late January."

"Seen Lonny lately?"

"This morning. That's when she cancelled today."

"So, Vix met her?"

"No." Jay narrowed his eyes. He had no intention of implying she'd spent the night with him.

Steve cleared his throat. "I've seen Lonny a few times recently. She's—I don't know—*nervy*. And she's drinking." He fingered his narrow goatee beard.

Jay shrugged. "When isn't she nervy?"

"I'm trying to be serious. It's not like Lonny to play hot and cold, but sometimes she looks through me like she can't see me."

Jay raised his eyebrows. "You know what she's like. She takes little offenses and magnifies them."

"Yes, I—"

The paint room door squeaked, and Vix emerged, her upswept hair falling around her face in soft curls. She aimed her gaze at Jay. "Cleaning up that place is going to take hours, but I can see I have the primary colors and don't need to buy anything but a few good brushes. Are you in charge of the key to this place?" She had a streak of blue paint on her yellow shirt.

"I'll get one cut for you tomorrow."

"Will you be here?"

He nodded. "We'll be starting at eight."

Trent threw the ball at Steve, who took it to the net. Vix lingered. "I don't have any painting to do yet, but I would really like to clean up the room. Would it be okay while you're working tomorrow?"

"Sure thing."

Sticky-beak Sherry insinuated herself between them. "Do you play volleyball, Vix?"

"No, I haven't ever played."

"You would be a natural." Jay glanced at her lithe body. "It's a game of tactics, and women seem to excel at that."

Vix dipped her head. "Tactics is a game I've yet to learn."

"One of them is to wear as little as possible," Sherry said, watching Steve and Trent remove their shirts. Since they knew she was watching, they smacked each other around. "Then the guys tip the ball low so that you have to bend over."

"Do you mean you do it on purpose?" Luke called from the other side of the room. He was shirtless and ready to play.

Sherry put her fists on her hips. "You're married. You shouldn't be noticing."

Vix looked at her own jeans and then at the brief outfits worn by Sherry and Kellen's two dates, all of which were tiny. While the guys had been setting up the net, the other three women had shucked off as many clothes as they could, leaving them in tight spandex undies and appetizer-type nipple coverings. "I won't be any use. I'm overdressed."

Everyone laughed.

"So, will you play?" Sherry asked, doggedly.

Jay didn't know why his sister-in-law was being pushy. She never bothered with Ilona, but most women didn't, which was a shame. That left Ilona with guys mainly, and a bit of female companionship would have done her a world of good.

"I'll watch for a while."

Jay found a gold throne in the props' room for Vix, and she sat backed against a fireplace flat while Trent formed groups inside the marks of Steve's hopeful boundaries, two guys and one girl a side, which left one of Kellen's girls wandering around and Jay sitting on the arm of the throne beside Vix. "In case you haven't guessed, we don't take this game too seriously."

"It looks seriously strenuous." She watched the leaps and catches with a half smile.

"They'll calm down as soon as they get into the game."

Without needing to be told, Kellen's date played using her own rules, distracting the guys on the other team with feminine ploys like adjusting bra straps or the flesh inside her bra. The guys on each team tried to distract the girls with ridiculous tricks, feints, and unlikely smashes. Jay saw the game as a mating ritual, as old as time, and, being the scorer, he gave points on the laughs rather than the balls hit.

"So, who won that?" Vix asked when Kell's girl retired, giggling.

"Trent's team."

Sherry folded her arms. "No way. You have to take off points for hitting other people with the ball."

"When did that rule happen?" Jay lifted his eyebrows.

"Today. The guys were showing off and that has to be penalized."

"I agree," Vix said, deadpan. "The game needs to be fair. The only people hit by the ball were female, and the only people hitting people with the ball were male, so in all, I think the women won." She tilted her chin.

"Let's have a challenge game of men against women, then." Jay rose to his feet and stripped off his shirt. He grinned at her. "Which means you have to play to make four a side. Who wants to sit out?"

Trent sat out, and he prowled among the stacked flats, choosing those he could knock apart and reuse while Jay got to play against Vix. His height gave him an edge and his strength proved most of his smashes winners, but he played harder that day than he ever had, whether to draw Vix's eyes or to work off tension, he couldn't say.

Without a scorer, no one won. No one cared. Kell's girls looked sweaty, and one draped her arm over his shoulders. The other, not to be outdone, snuggled up to his other side. Jay shook his head and caught Luke's eye. Luke shrugged.

"It must be lunch time." Sherry rattled around in her big shopping bag. "All that admiring of muscles has given me a huge appetite."

"Yeah, but for what?" Luke let a leering smile crease his face.

"Lunch. I've got three kids, in case you haven't noticed." She stood, a brown paper bag in her hands, clearly waiting.

Steve and Trent set up a couple of sawhorses near the opened big door and Kell topped them with a black masking flat. Sherry wandered over and unpacked the bag, placing thick sandwiches on the roll of kitchen paper she'd brought. The groupies had apparently been organized, too, and brought out plastic glasses and a supermarket cake. Kell supplied soda and lemonade.

Vix watched from a distance, looking like she thought she should leave.

"Are you going to stay for lunch?" Jay walked over to her and put his hands on her throne, prepared to move the monstrosity to the table for her to use if she chose.

She turned her head away. "I want to cover up that body of yours and hide it from view," she muttered.

"Whose view?"

"Mine."

He laughed. She wanted him. Perhaps she didn't know she did. All those orders she had given him last night might have put off another man, but not him. He didn't want to scare her. Ever. He could guess she'd been intimidated enough by her husband, who apparently didn't know how to make love to a young virgin, which she implied she had been when she married him. Apparently, Timmy-boy, a good ten years older than her, hadn't valued her as the prized possession she ought to have been.

"You should have more consideration," she said in a low voice. "You teased me all last night and now you want to do the same today."

"C'mere," he said gruffly.

She folded her arms.

He took a step into her and rested a hand on her shoulder. "What color are my eyes?"

"Denim."

"You'll have to learn to lift your gaze."

She stared straight at him. A pulse throbbed in her throat.

"Lunch it is, while I'm half-dressed and in full view."

She nodded.

"For now."

Her big eyes stared.

He'd begun to enjoy this new game and since he knew he couldn't do a bloody thing in the warehouse, he thought he might as well appreciate the anticipation. He wanted her and he would have her, but not with his friends around, and not until she was ready. His first time with her needed to be perfect, for her sake if not for his.

After examining his expression, she broke his hold.

He stared at her, noting her narrowed gaze. "If you don't want me, say so."

"You're getting really tricky now. You don't plan to touch me. I just can't work out why you want to make me think you do. If you're trying to be faithful to this Lonny, why not say so?"

"Don't you think it's more comfortable getting to know someone before you fall into bed with them?"

She tossed her head and the rest of her pencil-clasped knot of hair bounded in curls onto her shoulders. The pencil clattered onto the concrete floor. "If everyone knew everyone else, I think condom sales would take a dive. Knowing someone is the greatest deterrent to sex that I can think of." She bent to pick up her hair holder, apparently sure she'd had the last word.

"I don't think it hurts to see the color of someone's eyes first."

She put a finger in the middle of his chest. "Yours are green," she said, her voice husky. "A deep, dark, confident green and you have thick, girly eyelashes."

"We'll have to stop this." He stepped back. "And you can guess why."

Her eyes widened and she breathed out. "Here we go again."

He ate his doorstop sandwich, appreciating the fact that she had noticed the color of his eyes. She'd met his single stipulation. He didn't have to hold her off forever, as long as they could be very discreet. If Lonny found out, she would have a cow, but if Vix's father found out, he could produce a whole stampeding herd. James Tremain was one of the most powerful men in the state and once he'd had influence in Jay's life. Although the fight with Tim had ended that connection, he still had the power to mess with Jay's prospects. A smarter man than Jay wouldn't play with fire, but Jay didn't intend to be intimidated by money, now or ever.

He would like to be good enough for a woman like Vix, who was educated, quick-witted, earnest, fresh, clean, and wholesome. Just once he wanted to have a woman with inborn class. She played volleyball well, too, not like an athlete but like a fit, active woman. He liked that. Apparently, she'd spent the past year at the gym instead of mourning the loss of Tim. He liked that, too.

After the game, she went back into the paint room, he and the guys started shifting flats and reclaiming wood, and Sherry went home to the kids. Kell's girls huddled, possibly playing rock/paper/scissors to see who got the muscle-bound clod, though by now Jay knew the girls were friends who would leave the decision to fate, if that's what women did.

By the time he and the guys had stacked as much wood as they could, Vix had a pile of paint cans outside her room, and finally she emerged looking sexily flushed. She brushed her hands together, as if finished with the job. Her smile said satisfaction. "What's the rule for throwing out paint?"

"The same as for domestic dumping. You have to leave the paint to harden and then it's red-top waste."

"I can't reuse any of this, which is a shame because there's enough to paint a house."

"Mine needs painting."

She rested her forefinger on her chin. "What color do you want?"

"I don't care."

"There's not enough of a single color to do a whole room."

"I'll mix a few together so that I get enough."

"You ought to buy the colors you want. This lot mixed together will only make murk," she said, toeing a can. "Or, maybe…You could mix all of these greens with this dreadful yellow and get a quite interesting citrus green. Which room are you planning on painting?"

"All."

"Are you going to do up the whole of the inside of the house?"

"Sure. Eventually."

She gave him a delighted smile. "The house is yours, then. You have great bones there."

"Worst house in the best street in the worst neighborhood. But I got a good deal when I bought it. When I sell it, if the Port goes ahead as predicted, I might make some money. I sure could use some."

Her expression veiled. "Most people could. Anyway, I'm about to head off. Would you like me to give you a lift home? We live in the same direction."

He saw Steve and Trent were sitting on the floor, clearly ready to leave. "Yeah. We'll be starting at eight tomorrow. Right, guys? Let's go." He rattled his keys and the guys shuffled out of the door, last minute comments consisting of no more than "See ya."

Jay thought if Vix took him home, he could persuade her to stay the night. Maybe. She looked rather more businesslike now. Forever an optimist, he ushered her out to her car and piled in. As she backed her car out of the lot, he said, "Would you like me to cook tonight, or do you want to go out?"

"Sorry. I have work to catch up on."

The finality of her tone shot his eyebrows to his hairline. "So, I'll see you tomorrow?" Somewhere along the line, he'd erred, but he didn't know where. "What happened?" he asked, staring at her classic profile as she put the car into forward.

"Nothing, fortunately, as you know." Focused on the road, she began to drive like an elderly lawyer, slow and careful.

"I thought we had an understanding."

"No. You played with me, I played with you, and now we're even."

"You mean you had no intention of sleeping with me tonight?"

"No more intention than you meant to have sex with me last night." She laughed.

"Did you want to do it without a condom?"

"You had others."

"Watch out. That guy in front wants to change lanes."

She gave him *the look*. "You had a box in the bathroom."

"You're kidding. You went through my cabinet?" He tried to sound outraged.

Her cheeks tinged with red. "Do you know a woman who wouldn't?"

"I forgot I had condoms in the bathroom." The lie clogged his throat.

"Yet, that's where you went to get the one that you took into the bedroom to break in front of me. So, you really do care for the woman who came to see you this morning. Lonny, is that her name?"

"That's her name, and no, I'm not involved with her that way."

"Well, I just don't care what way you are involved with her." She took a right that led through the parklands to Port Road.

Although she might think she could put him off with her hauteur, he knew she would only have mentioned Ilona if she felt a tinge of jealousy.

And someone who didn't care didn't get jealous. "You don't have to take me home. You can stop here and I'll walk."

"Don't be huffy. It would take you a day and a half to walk to your house from here."

"You think I'm unfit?"

"I think you're narked." She gave a satisfied smile. "It's best this way, really. We have to work together and we need to keep our relationship on a purely professional basis." She lifted her lovely chin.

"You're right." He gave her a friendly smile, like he didn't care either. Normally, he wouldn't. At this stage of his life, a casual relationship suited him well enough, but she wasn't the sort of women he could be casual about. She was beautiful and broken and he knew his mending skills left a lot to be desired.

He let himself lose every emotion as she pulled up the car, her face guilty. She could stay guilty, though the blame for this slight interruption to a promising relationship could be placed at no one's door but his own. He scratched his ear as he watched her drive through the parklands and out of sight. Then, he turned and jogged back into the city to the car park nearest last night's venue, where he retrieved his motorbike, the overnight parking fee well worth having the excuse to get Vix to transport him twice.

Throughout his life, one step forward had always preceded two steps back. As usual, he would have to find a way of earning his second chance.

Bring on tomorrow.

Chapter 4

Vix had loved every second of the volleyball game yesterday—the physical activity and being with people her own age. She hadn't liked leaving JD to walk home, but she couldn't relent or he might think she would chase him, and of course she wouldn't. Bitter experience had taught her not to let a man dictate his terms to her.

Shadows still covered the parking lot when, dressed in her worst jeans and her oldest shirt, she pulled up her car outside the warehouse. Some people liked daylight saving, but she preferred her mornings where they ought to be, an hour later. Cold air chased her inside the building a little after nine. The place smelled of mold and sawdust and sounded like a day in hell with the bench saw shrieking in the distance.

Although she feared a slight awkwardness after her harsh assessment of him yesterday, JD, who had set up a long makeshift table near the light of the open doorway, lifted his gaze and gave her his big, tough-guy grin.

"Sleep well?" He had a pencil tucked behind his ear and his biceps bulged as he crossed his arms. Wood shavings clung to the front of his jeans and he wore heavy work boots and an open shirt, the sleeves rolled up.

Her lower belly reacted with a clench, but she was determined to show no reaction. "Like the dead." If she could maintain her assumed confidence, the friendly relationships she had been offered yesterday by people who teased each other, liked each other, and worked and played with each other, might not be withdrawn.

She hadn't had that sort of relationship with anyone in seven years. Marriage had taken her out of her world and into Tim's. Tim hadn't liked her childhood friends and so she'd contented herself with his friends, couples who drove fast cars, and judged clothes, restaurants, holidays, houses, and the quality of their children's education by price. Now, none knew what to do with his unrelenting wife when she refused all their invitations to spend her money. She didn't have the front to try to resume her older friendships when she'd been the one to end them...on Tim's insistence.

"I'll get a key cut for you later." He couldn't have looked more male as he bent to set out a few pages of diagrams.

Hoping she looked businesslike, too, she indicated her direction. "I'll be in the paint room if you want me." He gave her an eyebrow-raised smile and she swallowed, aware of her innuendo too late. She cleared her throat, knowing he didn't want her. "Figuratively speaking."

"What else?" He began to add to the pages with his pencil.

Although happy to admire his back view, she had work to do and so she slunk to the paint room, where yesterday's mess greeted her. In a way, she had already sorted out the paints. Her primary colors sat on the shelves, taking up more than one row each. Apparently the other painters didn't check the colors needed before they bought more, and so she had twelve tins of the same two blue mixers, none more than half-full.

Being boringly neat herself, she removed lids and began pouring from one can to the other. Aside from having a trail of blue paint from her wrist to her elbow and a blot under the sole of her left shoe, she ended up with five full cans of blue, three of one shade and two of the other, more than this production could ever possibly need. "You'd think I was a pauper," she muttered to herself, blotting her sleeve with a rag.

She did the same with the two shades of red and the two shades of yellow, and then she worked on the ochre and sienna, realizing that, unless she had miscalculated, she wouldn't need to spend a cent on paint. Saving money was one of her skills, weird when she'd never needed to.

Tim had married her for her family's wealth, but she hadn't known that in the beginning. She'd assumed he was also rich, which he could have been, but he thought he deserved the best of everything, a big house, expensive cars, and extravagant entertaining. Being "old money" herself, she was totally conservative. Her father had taught her to save money where she could. He even made his own wines. Watching Tim buy five-hundred-dollar bottles of French champagne to impress his friends, who drank the wine for the price rather than the taste, used to make her shudder.

Her marriage hadn't been made in heaven. Only the twenty-year-old optimist she'd been could have expected a happy-ever-after. Tim had been keen to use her money and her background, and she'd been dazzled by his flash, which had faded within a few months of marriage. She tried to tone him down and he tried to smarten her up. Instead of feeling comfortable in trophy-wife clothes, she ate. Instead of enjoying titillating positions in bed, she ate, for she was, of course, as sexless as he always said—a situation that would apparently never change. She blinked her eyes and straightened her mouth, which had a tendency to wobble during the odd recall.

Someone tapped on the door. She wiped her cheek with her sleeve. "It's not locked."

Sherry popped her head inside. Today she had her dark hair in a high ponytail, and she looked fresh and young in tight jeans with a blue cotton top. "Hi, Vix," she said, examining Vix's face. "I brought Luke's lunch. I didn't have fresh bread this morning and so he went without anything to eat. You're very quiet, packed away here by yourself."

"I would only be in the way out there."

Sherry drew her eyebrows together and patted Vix's hand. "Those guys make you feel like that, don't they? Men's men. Don't let them get to you. Luke's dad was a man's man. He didn't want his boys to be fairies. If it hadn't have been for Jay, they wouldn't have been anything but drunks like him."

"What did JD do?"

"He looked after Kell and Luke, although they're all two years apart, like my boys. JD's the oldest." Sherry widened the door to show a stroller with a small, freckled, redheaded boy in the seat and a dark haired, bigger boy holding the handle, or rather, swinging on the handle while he stared wide-eyed in the direction of the screaming saw. "Apparently their mum held the family together but after she died of breast cancer, their dad started drinking. JD would have been six or seven. He was eighteen when their dad died."

"And he looked after Kellen and Luke after that?"

"To keep it legal, they had an auntie who looked in occasionally but, yeah, he was the sole supporter. Lucky they owned the house. I don't know how you get a kid to look after two younger brothers. Mine sure doesn't, though he's only six. He's the first to ignore these two."

"He knows they're safe with you and Luke."

Sherry nodded. "Hope so. JD always used to scare me. He's, like, big and smart and you never know what he's thinking."

"The strong silent type." Vix half smiled. "But I don't see him as intimidating. He's been very friendly towards me." And she managed not to blush.

"You look like Lonny, but you're not like Lonny. He wouldn't want to scare a woman like you, but I didn't even finish high school. He didn't want me hanging around Luke because he wanted both his brothers to finish school like he did. Boy, was he mad when I got pregnant! But Luke married me and now JD accepts me." Sherry snatched at the arm of the boy who had been holding onto the stroller handle. "Noah, you can't go over there while the saw is working. When it's quiet you can go over to Daddy."

"What are their names?"

"Max, Noah, and Oscar. Oscar is the baby. Max is at school. Say hello to Vix, Noah."

The four-year-old gave Vix a considering stare. "Do you have a truck?"

"No. Does your daddy have a truck?"

"A pickup." The bench saw stopped and Noah glanced at his mother for permission before running over to the work area. "We brought your lunch, Daddy," he called in a high-pitched voice. "Mummy gave you cheese."

Luke appeared from behind the partition that only marginally kept the sawdust from the other parts of the room. The redhead spotted Sherry and she pushed the stroller over to him. He kissed her. Vix's throat thickened. Those two were younger than she was, but they had a family and a stroller and a pickup. She had paint cans and everything she wanted, except a family and a stroller and a pickup.

She didn't join them. So, she looked like Lonny, the friend Jay wasn't involved with that way, but she wasn't like Lonny. In what way? And should she be flattered or flattened? The break in the noise of the saw heightened her awareness of the voices, the shrill of the older child and the questioning tone of the younger, who stood precariously in the stroller, arms out, expecting to be lifted up by his father, who while talking to Sherry, did so.

Then JD arrived from the other side of the building, where she could hear low male voices, and took Oscar from Luke while Luke encouraged his look-alike son to help him shift a few pieces of wood into a neat pile. Vix watched JD. For some reason, the sight of a big strong man holding a small shy child made her blood race. JD couldn't have looked more masculine if he had flexed his muscles. His smile at the child glossed her eyes again. No doubt, all her sniveling today had been caused by the time of the month. She turned her back, determined not to yearn for the big strong man who hadn't, at any stage, flexed his muscles or done any more than tease her with a few placatory kisses.

She drew a deep breath and concentrated. Now having liters and liters of useless premixed colors to dispose of, she decided on conservation. At one stage, while she stood by the long bank of paint-spattered sinks at the back of the warehouse, the usual place for mixing or thinning paint, or for cleaning up, or whatever, she called to JD, who was opening packs of tech screws in the supply area. "Which room in your house would you paint green?"

He stared at her. "I don't think I would choose green."

"That's what I thought," she said glumly. "I can mix a couple of stunning greens but other than as a feature wall, I can't see where you would use green."

"Where would I want one as a feature wall?"

"In the back area. The wall that opens out to the garden, if you had French doors there that opened out."

"To a garden? Clearly, you haven't seen my backyard." He laughed.

She crossed her arms. "Would you want me to make a nice green for there, or not?"

"Sure. What color would the other walls be?"

"Do you want to go with the style of the house or modernize?"

Concentrating, he rubbed his chin. "Eclectic."

"Your floor would come up a lovely red brown if you polished it."

"I'm polishing the floor, too, am I?" His gaze questioned her.

"You'd be mad not to."

"Do I have to pay a consultant's fee for all this decorating advice?"

She smiled. "I can't stand waste. If I add a tad of red to the green, I think I can make an interesting beige, that is, if beige is ever interesting. There's so much white in some of these greens that it ought to work."

He lifted his eyebrows in an unasked question. "Luke and Sherry would like a yellowish green for one of the kids' rooms."

"I could make recycling old paint into a profession."

"You could. Will you be helping me do this painting you expect me to do?"

She sighed, glancing at the tins of paint. "If only I could say I don't have time."

"I could say I don't."

"I was waiting for that. I'll help you if you help, too." Her heart thudded. She had invited herself to his house and she had asked him to be present. Her faked confidence had perhaps taken her too far.

"When?"

"You're the one with no spare time." She turned her back, pretending to be absorbed in removing a can lid.

"Saturday?"

"Are you trusting me to choose the colors?"

"You're the expert."

"How long will it take you guys to make the house backdrop for the show?"

"I could mock-up a section today."

"Can I look at the plans with you?"

He nodded. "I can do whatever you want done first."

"I want the house first."

"Sounds like a woman."

She eyed him with a question. "In a divorce conversation? Yes, I got the house, but it was mine."

"Yep. Still sounds like a woman."

She let the conversation go. Her father had bought her house as a wedding present. Even Tim didn't have the front to try to claim it. No way would she let JD know how she had been used. And no way would she be used the same way again.

* * * *

Jay stretched his aching muscles when he heard the first ring of his phone. The second made him sigh. He knew without a doubt that Vix wouldn't be holding the receiver at the other end.

By concentrating on his work, he'd kept her out of his mind most of the day. Seeing her tomorrow would be tomorrow's problem. She had every quality he wanted in his woman. He saw only one drawback; she didn't notice any of his—really didn't notice anything but his body. He could give her pleasure, but that was all she wanted from him. And that wasn't enough, would never be enough for a man who was determined, despite every set back, to be more than his upbringing would normally have allowed.

"Hi, Lonny," he said, recognizing the caller number. He dropped a handful of detailed architectural drawings onto the couch.

"How's your presentation going?"

"Pretty near finished. I'm just completing the poster layout." He raised a palm to the ceiling, stretching slowly, easing the stiffness from his back. Building the set at the rate he'd been going took a toll on his body, though he kept fit by running when he had the time. "Thanks for the book on landscaping. I found it in the kitchen when I got home yesterday."

"I thought you'd be there. I thought that when I said I wasn't going to play volleyball, you wouldn't play either. I thought you'd rest instead." Ilona sounded hurt.

"Yeah, well, if I'd known that you were making a sacrifice for me, perhaps I would have." He subsided onto the couch, and single-handed, sorted through his drawings. He wanted to be sure he had chosen the right design.

"You're pathetic, Jay. You can't make me feel guilty. I don't make sacrifices and I never have. I was tired, that's why I didn't want to go."

"If you eased up on the night life a little, you might have the energy to do a few healthy daytime things."

"A fit mind in a fit body? I know your theory, but it won't work for me. I'm expected to be wherever the in-crowd is. When is your group presentation? Next week?"

"The beginning of next month."

"Can we have dinner on Wednesday night?"

"Sure. Where do you want to go?" He held up his first plan again, but no. The third was still the best.

"Maison Dee." Lonny said nothing for a few moments; then she sighed. "Do pasta. Something bland. Love you. See you Wednesday."

"Bye," he said, but she'd gone. For Ilona, conversations finished when she finished them.

After eating a slightly singed steak served with limp lettuce and a couple of tomatoes, he re-worked his computer model of sustainable apartments; then he went out for a run along the moonlit, rippling Port river, watching for the dolphins that often surfaced in the clear sea water. Not tonight, though. In the dark, he dodged dog-walkers and a few rough-sleepers and finally returned home, sweaty. Physically and mentally tired, he showered and swung into bed, expecting to sleep. Fortunately, he didn't mull over Vix for more than half an hour.

He drifted off formulating plans on how to keep eluding her. So far, that seemed to be the only way to maintain her interest.

* * * *

On Tuesday, Vix started painting the house-backdrop that would open the show and appear only then. The gracious house would fill the back of the stage, a house she would be slightly modifying from the original house in the Victorian production. The designer, who lived in Melbourne, had agreed that a direct copy was unnecessary, luckily, since Vix wanted to paint an American foursquare, which she saw as more appropriate for the wealthy family in the play; not only more traditional, but more difficult for her as a painter. She enjoyed a challenge and the '50s house in the movie had looked ordinary enough to have belonged to anyone.

Her *High Society* family was a little dippy. She laughed, knowing the play very well, and hoping the cast could manage the eccentricities required.

First, however, she needed to scale down the twelve by sixteen feet mansion and she did the work at home that night, sitting at her French antique desk whose patina was a joy to behold. Her whole study had been built to her specifications. Her leather chair molded exactly to her back and her footrest automatically adjusted to her position. She had no excuse to let her mind wander, but the memory of JD's big body easing between her legs made her tingle in that very place. But of course, if he belonged to another woman she had no right to those thoughts.

Something inside her chest twisted and she tightened her fingers around her pencil and concentrated. She expected to take most of tomorrow ruling up the panel he had constructed for her.

All she needed was a good ladder with a platform and she would be perfectly happy. Perfectly. Happy.

Chapter 5

"Do we have a platform ladder or do I need to buy one?" Vix stared at the messy paint-splattered wall on which a multifunction ladder and a combination extension ladder rested. A wooden stepladder painted black stood waiting to be tripped-over or walked into.

"We used to have one." Steve scratched his dark head, leaving his hair standing on end. "The sissy-ladder, Trent? Where did we put it?"

Vix sighed. The warehouse looked a mess. She could fall over almost anything from a hammer drill to a bundle of hessian, but she couldn't find a basic tool unless it was meant for tough guys. But she was a painter, not a cleaner, and she wouldn't tidy up a mess to which she hadn't contributed. "Why wouldn't you keep everything together?"

Trent put his hands on his hips. "We don't have time for housekeeping." His eyebrows lowered and he sounded outraged.

Vix had spent six years housekeeping and could understand why no one wanted the job she'd found far less mind-numbing by using a routine she never needed to change; tidiness, putting articles back where she found them, and finding logical places for everything. And so, with this in mind, she ignored logic and found the ladder she needed behind two black masking flats near the ghastly paint-spattered toilet block. If an element of being a sissy was to balance quite happily on a safe ladder, she would choose being a sissy any old day.

The whole place needed organizing, ladders with ladders, large flats standing along the walls at the back and smaller flats in front, wood in stacks kept with the composite sheeting in the building area, and broken furniture somewhere, *anywhere* else. If she were in charge, she would set everyone to doing that from the beginning. But she wasn't in charge, and she was a neat freak, and so she contained her frustration, setting up her ladder in front of her gigantic, composite-wood flat.

Within minutes, she was lost in her element, marking off, plotting, and drawing lines she constantly need to scribble out. Measure twice and mark once wasn't in her repertoire. She measured constantly and marked constantly, bearing in mind the scale of her drawings and her math, which was not her strongpoint. In the background, she could hear the guys talking and working, but she existed above their heads. She could hear their jokes, their camaraderie, and she belonged by not getting in the way.

She had noticed that the guys brought their lunches, and so she did, too. They ate thick sandwiches filled with meat or cheese, cold sausage rolls, scones or donuts, with nary a green leaf to be seen. She ate skinny sandwiches filled with salad and pieces of fruit. They eyed her food warily as if a vitamin might crawl out and bite them.

During breaks, she sat with them over mugs of tea, initially embarrassed by being the center of attention. She knew they carefully didn't swear in front of her, a courtesy she treasured. Her former crowd, Tim's smart friends, saw expletives as sophisticated when offered with a charming smile. She saw swearing as a waste of word time.

She hadn't been brought up to offend others, nor had she been brought up to see beauty in stick-like figures with faces plastered in makeup. She'd hoped beauty came from within. Only after she lost her husband and a quarter of her body weight had she paid more attention to her face and hair, and now men paid attention to her comments. Since she was exactly the same person, cynicism warred with enjoyment of her new guru status, which she'd assumed Tim's Ilona had been awarded because of her looks.

Making herself over in the image of the purportedly sexy blonde had been to show Tim that outward appearance could be manipulated by anyone who so chose. Anyone could have blond hair. Anyone could pile on makeup. Anyone could diet and exercise. In this effort to point out his foolishness, she'd gained new knowledge of herself. She had hidden behind her frump image deliberately when she had discovered she didn't like sex. Tim left her completely alone when she put on weight and he found someone else. His scathing attack on her sexuality had proved right, but she could live without sex, and had very gratefully during the past year.

Now she was caught in her own dilemma. She looked like a woman who might be sexually available when she very definitely wasn't. Until a few days ago, she didn't have a scrap of sexual awareness either, but that had changed on Saturday night when she met JD. She was now only too aware of him. The flesh on her cheeks warmed when she thought of him.

Her ladder trembled and she glanced down at his thick shaggy hair, his broad shoulders and his upturned, interesting face. "How are you planning to paint the stonework?" He had his foot on the bottom rung, and her complete attention.

"Painstakingly." She cleared her throat. Her hormones had gone wild and her hand shook. "I'm going to cut a stencil, which will take me all afternoon."

"Or all year, if you mean to make a stencil twelve feet by sixteen."

"Of course I don't. I will cut a small section and keep repeating the pattern."

"Do you want to use my table for cutting?"

"I can set up another."

"No need. I've finished with it. How about a lunch break?"

She stretched her back, so amazingly happy that she almost didn't know herself. JD would never be Tim. JD was not just interested in sex. He was interested in tasks, who could do what and how. He made even her job relevant. He would never be the center of attention; people would never speak of him in hushed whispers or give him the benefit of the doubt. He would never spend hours on his dressing or in front of the mirror. He didn't need to. He was a man with a tall, fit body, a careless, sexy walk, and a smile that warmed a woman's body.

He could do more for her libido during a few second's conversation than Tim could do in a year. She breathed out, glad to find that she actually had a libido to dither about. "Would you like to see the green I mixed for your feature wall?" she asked, her face warming with her thoughts.

"I don't have an eye for color. Surprise me on Saturday." He waited for her to descend the ladder. "Do you want me to make windows in your house flat?"

She shook her head. "Real windows will make the rest look fake. I want to paint it all in a realistic way."

"Be sure you plan for pillars outside that turret, then."

"I have." She scrutinized her big, half-finished sketch on the flat. "Should I do marble pillars, do you think, or the rough-cut stone ones I'll be putting either side of the porch?"

"Marble."

While she ate her sandwich, she watched him. He leaned back, confident of himself and his work. The others didn't question his orders. They asked for his advice. The man was a natural leader.

And, amazingly, he agreed that her stone foursquare mansion would look far better with marble rather than rough-cut pillars between the upper windows and fronting the third story.

* * * *

"Is fettuccine carbonara bland enough for you?" Jay stood back, waiting for Ilona to enter the house.

"And good evening to you, too." She stepped into Jay and hugged him, elbows around his neck, her body a little too snug against his. "Carbonara sounds perfect," she said, her breath tickling his ear. "I brought a bottle of red, a Maintree."

He set her aside, taking the bottle. "You're looking good."

She lifted back her long blonde hair. "You're looking hot, and I don't mean warm-hot." With a heavy-lidded glance up and down his length, her version of sexy, she turned and made her way into his kitchen.

He followed with the bottle, cracking the seal while she reached into an upper cupboard for two wine glasses.

"Steve said you found a blonde for the volleyball game. Who is she?" She held out her glass for him to fill.

Jay shrugged. "The set painter."

"Trust you to combine work and play."

He lifted his eyebrows. "Who says I did?"

The color of her eyes changed from caramel to black. "Instinct. I'm pretty sure I walked in at a bad time on Sunday morning." She looked as eye-catching as usual, wearing long silver earrings with a figure-hugging gray dress.

"No worse than at any other time." He gave a wry grin.

"You were loving up your blonde, that's why you wouldn't let me come into the bedroom." She gathered her hair in a bunch, a restless habit like her next fiddle, which took the lot over her right shoulder, where she combed her over-gilded locks with her fingers. This meant that the next time she moved, her hair would cover two shoulders and her back. Then, within minutes, the whole routine would begin again.

"Nope." Jay filled her wine glass to the brim, and trickled an inch into his. "I was asleep until I heard you call out."

"I bet you screwed her all night long."

"No." He took a saucepan from the cupboard. "Not that it's any of your business."

"Okay. I get it. The subject's closed," Ilona said in a sulky voice as he filled the saucepan from the sink tap. "It's not as if that particular subject has ever been open. You've never talked about your sex life. I'm the one who does, always wanting your advice about this man or that man. You never comment one way or the other."

"You're a big girl, Lonny. I think you can make your own decisions."

She toyed with the keys he had left on the counter top. "In the whole world, I think you're the only person I trust. I felt the same way about you when we were younger. I punished the other boys with sex, but not you."

He added a pinch of salt to the water. "Trust me. None of them feels punished."

"Thirteen-year-old girls don't know too much, no matter how sophisticated they pretend to be. I had to be tough, and you know why."

"Yeah, I know. Your mother's bastard boyfriend raped you."

"Legally, but technically I consented, which even now makes my flesh creep." She took a mouthful of wine, swirled the fluid around and swallowed. "I thought I was a grown woman and grown women let men do things like that. The child protection services would have taken me away from Mum if I'd said anything, and no matter how lax my mother was, she was all I had... until you took over and let me join your gang. In all that time, nothing has changed. I still hang around, I still try to get your advice, and I still love you."

He swiveled to face her, wondering what she wanted from him. She rarely brought up the old days and she didn't have a sentimental bone in her body. Finally, he nodded. "What's this about?"

Her gaze flickered over his face and she took another large glug of her wine. "Hey, this wine's good, even if I do say so myself. It's an exclusive one I got from Tim."

Jay waited for her to lift her gaze, but she kept toying with the keys as if she was deciding what to say. Finally, he picked up his glass and took a taste, trying a swill around his mouth, too, acting like a connoisseur, but he didn't have taste buds that cared. "Since you say so, it must be."

She forced an overdone sigh, indicating that whatever she had been about to confide was now safely tucked away in the place she called "forget it." That's what she did when she thought she couldn't get what she wanted—pretend she didn't want it. He knew her too well. He turned to put the saucepan on the hob.

The keys clattered onto the laminate. "I don't know why I bother bringing wine around here," she said in a petulant voice. She brushed past him to drag out the cutlery drawer from which she took out two forks.

"I can't afford to be a drinker, not with my family's background."

She pushed back past him to clatter the implements onto the gray table. "Just because your father was a drunk doesn't mean—"

"It means I don't want to be like him. And it means I don't want you to be like him, either. Slow down. There's always tomorrow."

"Thankfully. Because I'll be drinking tomorrow, too, if I feel like it."

Jay shrugged. Over the years, he'd discovered that any criticism of Ilona made her go the other way. He wished he hadn't said anything because she tossed down her wine faster than he could breathe. He refilled her glass, sniffed his thyme-flavored bacon and mushroom sauce, and turned on the oven to heat the garlic bread. "Put on some music."

She walked over to the old cupboard on the farthest wall and opened out two tall doors, exposing the old stereo, the speakers, a few CDs, and overhead shelves stacked with books, mainly library loans. Within minutes the thud of a metal band saturated the room, too loud, the way Ilona liked music. He didn't care. With her in a tricky temper, he would rather listen to music than flounder with her moods.

He served the pasta. When she'd eaten half, she pushed her plate away with a wrinkling of her nose.

"Perhaps now you can tell me what's griping you and get it over with."

Her dark eyes connected with his. "I did something I swore I would never do and now I'm regretting it."

"That's a breakthrough on two levels." He grinned at her.

She grabbed her hair and settled the bunch on her right shoulder, again. "I've had regrets before. I just don't admit to them. And." She drew a breath. "What would you say if I asked you to make love to me?"

"You know what I would say. Why would you ask?"

Without meeting his gaze, she shook her head. "Testing. I need to know that you are you," she said in a low voice.

He nodded slowly. "The same as you are you. Always testing, never trusting. You're my friend, Lonny. You always will be. You don't need to lure me with sex."

"I know." She turned her fork end over end and straightened. "So, how's the set doing? Who's helping you build this one?"

He took a moment to deal with the swift change of subject before answering. "Trent took time off to help me, and Steve recently finished another job, so he's with me until a few weeks after Christmas. Kell has a kitchen to finish, but he'll help later. Why do you ask?"

She pushed the remains of her food around her plate with her fork. "I might want some new partitions built in the salon. Will you let me have one of your trusty team for the job?"

"We're pushed for time as it is. I might be able to free up Trent, but I think you should ask Kell. He could knock up partitions for you in his workshop and fit them in a day."

"In a day?"

"Straight-out partitions? He might even paint them as well if you ask nicely."

"I've been known to ask nicely, on occasion." She rose to her feet and took the plates to the kitchen area.

He followed. Together they washed and dried the dishes while she discussed her rebuilding plans with him. The whole time they talked, he wondered what she had to regret and why she had tried to sidetrack him with the old sex debate. Even years ago, when he had been young and randy, he hadn't accepted any of her offers. She thought she had to buy love with sex. He wanted her to see herself as worthy of friendship.

Finally he put two mugs of coffee onto the low table in front of the couch. She chose another CD, which she played loud enough to vibrate his eardrums. He softened the volume. She jutted out her lower lip, crossed her arms, and sat there, staring at him. Her eyes looked over-bright.

"C'mon." He reached out to her and took her into his arms, pressing her head to his shoulder. "Tell me your problem. I'm here for you, as always."

One of her hands reached to the hair on the nape of his neck. She pulled her fingers through as if soothing herself, but still she didn't say a word. He touched his lips to her forehead.

"Let it out," he said, holding her as he had so many times before, against his chest with one hand stroking lightly over her upper arm.

She took a breath, which she released in a long sigh while she snuggled closer to him. "Do you see me as a woman or a friend?" She folded a pleat into the front of his shirt.

"I see you as a woman friend."

She hid her face in his shirt. "I've never had a proposal of marriage. I'm twenty-nine. I don't want to be single forever."

"If that's all you want, no problem. Steve would propose any time you hint you might listen."

"Well, I wouldn't listen. I wouldn't marry a loser who barely knows how to keep himself off the dole."

"He makes a very good living now."

Her fingers tightened into the shirt fabric over his chest. "Not good enough. I want someone who makes more money than I do. You understand the need for security," she said, staring into his eyes.

"I do. I make my own—and I wouldn't marry for money."

"A real man wouldn't." She pushed away from him. "You're a real man. That's what I want."

"There are plenty out there waiting for a woman like you."

"I've been out there and I can't find one."

"You're looking in the wrong places."

"When you want rich, you move in those circles."

He hauled in a breath. "Perhaps you ought to have stayed with Timothy Nolan. From what you're saying, he's the man for you."

"He didn't want marriage." Her face hardened. "He wanted sex."

"He had a wife." He lifted his eyebrows.

"She wouldn't let him touch her."

"If a man can't get sex from his woman, she doesn't want him, which it seems his wife proved by divorcing him."

"He divorced her and she took just about everything he owned including the house," she said with contempt. "Leaving him with not quite as much money as I expected. Maybe her greed put him off marriage, who knows? I don't care. He was hell in bed."

His neck stiffened. "He was violent?"

"Inadequate. He needed to be turned on. I don't want to talk about him anymore." Her expression a challenge, she slipped her fingers past the buttons of his shirt and began caressing his skin.

He put his hand over hers, stopping her. "Cut that out. I might be more susceptible than you think."

"Let's find out."

He shook his head. "Neither of us needs to prove a thing."

Her eyes filled with tears. "You bastard. I need to prove I'm attractive. Can't you see that?"

"Can't you see you are? You're good looking and smart. It's time you stopped selling yourself short."

"I'm bad. Look what I did to you." Her gaze focused on his scar. "You got that because of me."

"I'm not into victim blaming. I got that because your ex-boyfriend was jealous. He thought I was his competition. I don't think for a minute he expected to mark me like this and if he hadn't been wearing that signet ring, I would only have been bruised."

"You should have hit him back."

"In hindsight, yes. I didn't know he would use the buddy system to get my scholarship withdrawn."

"And if he hadn't thought you were his competition, you'd have a guaranteed job at Tremain's next year."

He sat, his hand on her hair, recalling the night he'd spent in custody thinking he'd been a white knight, only to discover that witnesses said otherwise, as did the court. His scholarship, his only means of support, had been revoked and his need for a job had lost him his place at the university, which he had taken back part-time the next year. "Strangely, I don't regret a thing. I'm almost there now, despite the detour, and I've learned a lot along the way. It's no disadvantage to know a little about construction before getting an architectural degree."

"I'm sick of making other people look beautiful. Could you use me in your set-making team?"

His mouth dried. He didn't want her around, not with Vix. Lonny was hell on other women, and he doubted Vix could handle Lonny's brand of competition. "Not unless you're good with a miter-box."

"I can manage a paint brush."

"No you can't, Lonny. You do a couple of strokes and then you want someone to clean your brush, or set up a roller. You're in the business that suits you best and you know it."

She heaved a sigh. "What are you doing on Saturday?"

"I'm helping someone paint a room."

"I meant on Saturday night."

He wiped his palms down his jeans. "Same thing."

"Can I stay over, tonight? I just don't want to be alone."

Almost relieved, he said, "Sure. Your bedroom is still the way you left it."

"You won't let me sleep with you?" She looked at him from under her lashes. "I want comfort."

"It's not a good idea."

"You're afraid to share a bed with me." She stood, hands on her hips, chin defiant. "You think you'll want me if you do."

He inclined his head to the side and stared at the stunning blonde. "I think it's more important to you and to me that I don't use you. If you can't see that, you don't understand our relationship."

"You're right. I don't." She threw down her wine as if he'd challenged her. "But you don't either. I could make you want me, you know."

Chapter 6

In the morning, Vix pulled up her Mercedes in the concrete car park outside the warehouse. Luke's scruffy white pickup sat beside Steve's flashy white four-wheel drive, which transported the rest of the team to work in the mornings.

Vix didn't like the look of her shiny new black car beside the others. She didn't like that she had purchased the Merc after her divorce merely to annoy Tim, who had wanted this particularly pricey model. Her money hadn't been made by her but by her ancestors, and she would feel more pride in a car she had bought with her own hard work. Since she hadn't yet earned any money, she decided to trade down, a deed her father wouldn't question. Nor would he care what sort of car she drove. He had always despised ostentation for himself, while making sure he pressed the biggest and the best upon his only daughter.

Feeling ostentatious and consequently chastened, she walked inside the echoing building, seeing no one, but hearing voices from the back. To make her presence known, she proceeded toward the source and heard Steve say from behind the bench saw partition, "He's screwing her. There's no doubt of it."

"If so, it's his business, not yours," Trent said, sharply.

"Maybe, but why does he lie about it?"

"P'raps he doesn't want to hurt you."

"Like I give a freakin' damn."

The band saw started screeching, and a length of wood clattered onto the floor. "...was her car in his driveway this morning," Steve yelled above the noise. "And you saw her come out and wave him off. Nothin's surer than she stayed the night."

Determined not to be an eavesdropper, Vix walked behind the partition, and said, "Good morning. How's everything going?"

The two men looked up. "We're making the poolside huts today," Steve said, his face tight and his voice terse. "Luke's working on the pool. JD is working on the balustrade for the terrace."

"Fantastic." Stepping backward to avoid a cut length of wood on the floor, Vix awkwardly knocked into a half-made flat, which teetered until she grabbed one end. "I'm off to finish painting the house." She held the flat until the edge stopped trembling, and didn't look up until she could smile brightly.

Even someone as credulous as she could make a logical assumption about who the guys were talking, because Steve always stopped to pick up JD. Her cheeks hot with hurt and embarrassment, she mixed ochre and white to make the stone color for the mansion.

So, she had thrown herself at a man who wasn't available. Worse was still being so attracted to him, but why not? The man was every good girl's dream, sexually responsive rather than being sexually available. He would never push his own needs. As she rolled the entire flat with the undercoat, she steeled herself into seeing him as he was, an attractive man who didn't want to alienate a workmate, which she had scrupulously been since the embarrassing beginning and which she would be certain to remain from now on.

While she waited for the finish to dry, she inspected the stencil she had made at home last night, a tracery of cut-out blocks, checking her measurement against the front section of the house. With the stencil repeated, she would end up with three quarters of a block on the corner of the so-called building, which would certainly not look like a corner edge on a real house.

Sighing, she sat at JD's table with his pencil in her hand. Only a miniscule adjustment to the porch area was required to fix the problem. Three times she did the math, and three times she came up with different measurements. In the distance, the guys talked, argued, drilled holes, banged in nails, and laughed. Her own space echoed with her frustration. She would have to make a whole row of faux cut stone smaller than the rest. Probably no one would ever notice but knowing that left her with an uncomfortable niggle of frustration. For her first job, she wanted to produce something spectacularly right.

Restless, she rose to her feet and strode to the tiny kitchen at the back of the building, where she and the guys usually sat for their breaks. She filled the urn, which she turned on. Last night she had made a cake for morning tea. JD's active sex life wouldn't be allowed to ruin her day. Nor would the guys' attitude towards sissies. She didn't like sitting in a mess, and she wouldn't.

Mouthing the words to Pink's "Stupid Girl", she set the table with a sissie's tablecloth, set out plates, and lined up the various mismatched mugs. "Maybe if I act like that, flippin' my blond hair back..." danced her to the doorway, where she yelled, "Morning tea is served, gentlemen."

All noise ceased. Fortunately, a silence couldn't really deafen, and she heard a laugh. Then a single male voice called back, "Okay."

She waited, horrified. Instead of thinking the song, she had yelled the words. While she heard the tools being tossed down, the murmur of conversation, and the approaching footsteps, she poured the milk from the carton into a sissie's jug. "So there," she muttered, slicing the cake into man-sized chunks.

One by one, the guys arrived, stared at the table, made a hot drink, and sat, JD last. This was her first sight of him today and he looked gorgeous, clean and hunky, and so sexy that she didn't doubt he'd been satisfied in bed last night. By a real woman, Lonny the magnificent.

Vix folded her arms, determined not to show her feelings. "One sexist comment from anyone and I don't share my cake."

"I love the flowery tablecloth," Trent said, alerting her with a wide-eyed grin. "Our Nan had one just like it."

"Shouldn't we use spoons to eat the cake?" Steve lifted his mug, prissily curling his little finger.

"Forks," Luke said, a frown on his freckled face. "Little ones. Sherry and I got some for a wedding present. Maybe I ought to bring them tomorrow."

"The cake will be stale tomorrow. I'm sure Vix will let you use your hands today." JD's khaki eyes met hers and her chest thumped loud enough to hear.

She tilted her chin. "As it happens, I brought cake forks."

Four pairs of eyes turned toward her in horror, and she laughed. "Kidding. It's orange and poppy-seed cake. I hope you like it."

She drank her tea, knowing that not only couldn't she and JD be lovers, they didn't have enough in common to be friends. Although he could make a woman's body hum, that was of no use to anyone but his girlfriend. Discussing the classics with a tradesman would be a waste of time. All he and she could talk about was sets. Nevertheless, when she looked at him, her body craved. He knew how to tease a woman until she wanted to tear off his clothes and run her hands all over his skin.

Lucky Lonny. She had a man who could pin her body with his, smile, and give her hard/soft kisses and pretend he wanted her, though in Lonny's case, he wouldn't need to pretend. Nor would he need to understand why a woman who'd been belittled by a control freak would not let another man guide the sex play. A macho male like JD would see Vix's orders as he did; a slur on his masculinity. She knew why he had destroyed the condom but aside from having a trusting girlfriend, Vix's insecurities would have put him off.

Morning tea over, she heaved a breath and stood. "Back to the drawing board," she said, with a frustrated sigh.

JD raised his eyebrows. "Having a problem?"

"What makes you assume that?"

"Your tone of voice, Michaela-Angela. Can I help?"

"Only if you know how to work a slide rule," she said in a superior voice, dusting the crumbs of the cake into the bin.

The guys all paused, waiting, strange expressions on their faces.

JD stared at her, pushed his hands in his pockets, and said, "Actually, I do."

And so, after a slight adjustment in two places across the width of the porch, Vix finally began forming her perfectly matched stone blocks.

* * * *

Jay felt like a heel. He hadn't counted on Lonny standing in his doorway this morning, waving him off like a wife sending her husband to work with a packed lunch. Normally, instead of eating breakfast, she spent at least an hour in the bathroom, plastering on her makeup and styling her hair to look exactly the same as when she had crawled out of bed. He also hadn't given a thought to her car parked out the front for Steve to see. Steve had always been possessive of Lonny, although he knew, like JD, that most of his friends had had sex with her at one time or another.

This also gave Jay a guilt trip. For years he'd told himself that he was Lonny's friend and friend-sex simply wasn't on. Last night he'd realized, when she said she loved him, that although his long friendship, or guardianship, gave him feelings for her, too, she had never featured in his mind as a sexual being. Even if she had, he wouldn't want a woman who'd had sex with his friends any more than he would want to join the queue. He'd turned out to be a prissy-mouthed hypocrite despite all his noble speeches.

After checking his diagrams for the size of the trapdoor in the stage floor from which the pool would appear when needed, he put a steadying knee on the sawhorse and cut an angle into the bull-nosed length of wood, which Vix would paint as a stone edge. She was back on her platform ladder again, this time marking out windows for her three-story house.

From where he stood, her stonework looked real. At some stage, she had blotted ochre and gray onto her fake stone, unevenly, adding light and shade for depth, and the whole sat together well. Too bad she was lousy at calculations. He smiled to himself. She would need him again, and soon, because her windows didn't fit proportionally under the turret. He watched her descend her ladder and stand back, narrow-eyed, assessing the mistake he had spotted.

She turned and glanced at him. Then she raised her chin, flipped back her blond hair, climbed up the ladder, and re-marked correctly. His mouth relaxed. Today she wore her paint-smeared jeans that did wonders for her curvaceous behind. Her big shirt hid the rest of her, but he knew how she looked. He knew she had smooth-skinned, firm breasts, a supple waist, and a muscle-flat belly. He wanted her, and he set his mind to achieving his aim on Saturday…if she could be convinced he would be good for her.

The sheets of corrugated iron wall began to protest the afternoon temperature drop and he glanced at his watch. Work started at eight and the team liked to leave by five. The sounds of packing up for the day began, the clattering of a wood length thrown on top of others, the rattling roll of the stack collapsing under the weight, a curse, and flats thumped upright against the walls. Male voices murmured. Footsteps clumped to the kitchen and back, the broom handle bounced on the floor, all familiar sounds, along with the metallic click of tools being locked back into metal boxes.

Vix glanced around, clearly brought of out her focused painting world and into the present. She'd marked out the panes in her two sets of two big windows on one side of the building. On the other, she'd sketched a front door with two tall, rough-cut pillars on either side. On the veranda above stood another four pillars. These were smooth marble, or would be, he assumed. Higher still was the turret, as yet only windows and stone.

After a blink at him, she took her brushes off to the sink area. He packed up while he waited for her to return, which she did, wiping her wet hands down the sides of her jeans. "See you tomorrow," she said, grabbing up her big workbag. Diagrams poked out at the top, drawn with colored pencils, and a white plastic ruler rested on top.

"I won't be here tomorrow." He brushed the sawdust off his shirtfront. Her eyes followed his hands, showing an unconscious interest in his body.

"A day off after three days work?" she said in a cynical voice, her gaze meeting his as the guys ambled over.

"He takes a day or two off every week." Luke grinned at him. "He's what you might call an unsteady worker."

Jay silenced his brother with a look. "Any problems, see Steve. He's in charge when I'm not here. Are you okay with that, Steve?"

"Me?" Steve sounded pleased. "No worries."

Jay trusted Steve as a good steady worker, and Jay had decided to interfere in Lonny's life. The set-building team would need another boss when he left after this job. Steve, like any other builder, relied on the economy for the bigger jobs. At times, he had to take work interstate. This caused him to mumble and grumble about not being able to settle down. If he had a regular business of his own, taking on a mortgage wouldn't be a problem. The set-building team, under a new management that didn't have other plans, could expand into other areas like temporary venues for festivals, outdoor concerts, or large events. Then Steve would earn more money than Lonny, and she might consider a man who loved her as her partner, rather than one who had only lately begun to judge her.

Arriving home, he cooked and ate a stir-fry, and moved the furniture from his sitting-slash-dining area into the hall. He then proceeded to knock every nail in the floor below the level of the wood. Next step was to putty the holes and he had that done in an hour.

Tomorrow, after he and his fellow architectural students had delegated the order of speaking for their final presentation, he would check his computer models as well as his programs predicting the thermal properties of his designs. That done, he could get back to work on his own home.

He planned to hire a floor-sander and go over the floorboards tomorrow night. He could add a couple of coats of sealer on Friday, and by Saturday he would have a finished floor to show Vix that he wasn't a complete loser. She already liked him enough to offer to help him paint. If she liked him more, she might be willing to snuggle into his arms and kiss him back.

He eased into bed, tired but smiling.

* * * *

Without JD at work, the guys messed around, going from one task to the next without finishing anything properly. JD might have had a steadying presence, but apparently not a work ethic, which surprised Vix. When he bothered to turn up, the set progressed smoothly without the questioning of plans or the hunt for drawings to check on the measurements that Steve constantly disputed with Vix. Women, apparently, didn't understand the finer points of carpentry or the myriad of uses for duct tape.

She painted window frames and panes on the house flat. She tiled the three separate roofs, figuratively speaking. She added a painted set of glass-paned mahogany front doors, brass handled, and, after a squinty-eyed examination, decided she'd caught the gleam of the metal rather well. Then, she marbled the four colonial pillars along the upper veranda and the four under the turret roof. Unable to restrain herself, she painted three aqua-blue window boxes filled with red geraniums, which she had mocked up on her thick stenciling paper, and stuck these between the turret pillars. Laughing, because she loved the light-hearted '50s look but knew the set designer wouldn't allow her to use her own ideas, she took a photo with her phone and sent it to him.

He answered back in fifteen minutes. *Gorgeous, darling.*

She texted, *Can I keep the boxes?* and she waited half an hour, nervous, although she need not be. The window boxes could be removed with a grab.

You may, said his next text, and she jumped for joy. She wished JD had been there to see her triumph.

The guys stared at her as though she was crazy.

"It looks nice," Steve said, scratching the back of his neck. Among his forearm tattoos was a large fish on a hook, a heart with an arrow, and a dragon eating its own tail. "I don't know why you thought the designer wouldn't like it."

"Well." She chewed her lip. "It's my idea."

"I've seen window boxes before."

"It's meant to be a gracious house for rich people."

"It's three stories with marble pillars. I think you have represented that," he said loftily. He folded his arms and blotted out the sight of a skull with a rose for an eye. "Have you seen the show?"

"I saw it a couple of months ago in Melbourne, when I was applying for this job."

"So, what's the deal with the changing-huts? They're kinda useless around the pool when the back door of the house is only a few steps away."

She lifted her hands, to help with her explanation. "They're mainly to show the wealth of the family but... Do you know the story?"

"The story of a musical? Where people talk for a couple of minutes and then they start singing at each other or break out into a gay little dance? Not on your life." He planted his fists on his hips.

She grinned. "The leading lady is about to get married, but she isn't sure that she is marrying the right man. The night before her wedding, she drinks too much and takes a swim in the pool. When she wakes up next morning, she's wearing a man's toweling robe and nothing else, and she finds a man's watch in the pocket."

"So, she swam naked," Steve said, his gaze on hers.

"She doesn't remember, but clearly she wasn't skinny-dipping alone and this is the night before her wedding. Her husband-to-be wasn't a houseguest. Because of the changing-huts, the audience saw how she happened to be wearing the wrong robe."

"She did the fandango with another guy?"

"The only person who believes she didn't is the man who loves her."

"That'd be the man she was with."

She shook her head. "He was too sozzled to remember what happened, as well."

Steve scratched his head and without another word went back to making the doors for the changing huts. She started on the stonework surrounding the pool, wishing she wasn't glad that tomorrow she would be seeing the man who was probably with the woman he kept denying he was with.

* * * *

Jay slid into the back seat of Steve's car in the morning. A streamer of gray smoke wound in two veins through the lapis lazuli sky. A sunny day was forecast. The early morning light cast bleak shadows across his garden, the piled soil dry and the weeds continuing to multiply. For the past two years, he had been time poor. "Good morning, guys."

"Seems we're making a set for a show about rich people sleeping around," Steve said to the rear vision mirror, catching Jay's reflected glance.

"They didn't have sex in the '50s." Jay settled back into his seat belt.

"So, how did our parents get born?"

Trent clipped Steve upside the head. "Moron. They only pretended they didn't have sex."

"Pretty stupid thing to pretend when everyone would know when the kids were born."

Jay sighed. The day would be long. "Have we finished the poolside scene yet?"

"Vix's painted the pool. She'll be doing the changing-huts next. Seems they got up to a fair bit of sex in those."

"Wall-banging sex. There's no room to move in those little huts." Trent rolled his shoulders and turned slightly to grin at Jay.

"Today is going to be all about sex, is it?"

"See Lonny yesterday?" Steve said, jerking a left to join a gap in the Commercial Road traffic.

"Speaking of sex? No, I didn't and, no, I haven't had sex with her. Ever. Won't. How about if you make a move, Steve, since you're so obsessed?"

Steve pulled to a screeching halt at the traffic lights. Jay's seatbelt bit into his chest. The floor sanding yesterday had taken him four hours.

The cleaning up had taken another hour. His arms ached from holding the bucking machine steady all that time. He didn't doubt the work would be worth the effort. The floor could have been done months ago, but he'd clearly lacked the motivation to knock himself out. Now he had a good reason to tidy up the house. Vix.

Weird that he wanted to impress her. A wrong-side-of-the-tracks guy like him couldn't impress a girl with class and he could bet his lack of car and his work-in-progress house didn't impress her much either. She'd been pretty cool with him on Wednesday.

He strode into the warehouse with a loss of confidence not natural to him. Maybe the house-painting session was off. By the time she turned up at nine, he was dry-mouthed nervous. "Hey," he said, tucking his thumbs in the waistband of his jeans.

"Hey. What are you making today?"

"I'll be starting on the kitchen flat." He walked over to her, noted her glossy high ponytail, her clear pink lipstick, smelled her perfume, and practically salivated. "Look over this plan. Do you want the window built into this or do you plan to paint one?"

"Paint one. Will the flat be flown or entered from the side?"

"Flown."

"I love the window in the kitchen. It's the feature."

"Looks pretty much like the outside windows."

She gave him a lowered head glance. "In some houses, the windows on the outside connect to the inside."

"Yeah, even in mine. Speaking of which, what time are you coming tomorrow?" He held his breath.

"Tomorrow?" She frowned. "Tomorrow's Saturday."

"To my house for painting."

"Oh. I forgot. You want me to help paint. I can come sometime in the afternoon."

"How about midday? I'll make you a sandwich and we can discuss the division of labor."

"What sort of sandwich?"

"Would vegemite make this a deal-breaker?"

"I could..." she began and stopped, narrowing her eyes at the expression on his face. "Very funny. Okay, I'll trust you as to sandwiches, which is only fair because you are trusting to my color sense. I'll see you at twelve, then."

He whistled while he worked, trying to remember a time when he had looked forward to working on a Saturday afternoon.

Chapter 7

Already late, Vix still hadn't decided what to wear. Jay had seen her in work clothes since the night they had met and she wanted to look a little more special than a scruffy painter. With only painting to do, she couldn't think how she could look any better. Everything she'd tried on so far either looked too careful or a little provocative. During her marriage, she had preferred to look invisible, but since she'd lost weight, she'd only bought clothes designed to attract attention.

With a sigh, she slid a red spotted top—one that covered her from the top of her shoulder blades to her hips—over her head, and she pulled on jeans unmarked with paint. JD wouldn't notice she had tried because she looked only a tiny bit neater than on weekdays.

Brushing her hair into a topknot, she regretted almost asking herself into his home. What would she talk about? She only knew how to discuss sets with him.

When she stopped the car in his driveway, he came outside. He had pulled most of his thick hair into a band on the top of his head, too. His shaggy fringe remained and for the first time she noticed his chiseled cheekbones. He stood, his hands in the back pockets of his jeans, which over time had developed worn areas on the knees and the thighs. Today he wore kung-fu shoes instead of work boots and a T-shirt instead of a working shirt, and he looked absolutely delicious, especially with his hair out of the way.

"New car?" He lifted his eyebrows.

"New path?" She lifted hers.

He had removed the delivered wood and had neatly smoothed the piles of soil in the front garden, making the walk to the front door look less hazardous.

"What was wrong with the Merc?"

"Nothing. It was a nice car, but it had to go back to the owner." Technically, her father was the owner, and he had sent a broker around with the car she now drove, taking away the Mercedes. "I got this instead. What do you think?" Grabbing her bag and a collection of new paintbrushes, she swung out of the driver's seat.

"It suits you."

She smiled, surprised. "As a matter of fact, it does. It's really light to handle and it has a tiny turning circle. I'm not sure about the color, though. It's a bit bright."

"It's your color. And yes, I am thinking about the new path. I'll do the paving as soon as I have time. I might have to do some planting first. The weather's right, or so I heard on the radio this morning. Let me grab those roller trays." With an armload, he led the way to the house and picked through the furniture he had stacked into the hallway.

When she reached the kitchen/dining area, she stopped. "Wow!" The floor glowed smooth and shiny, the color ranging from light pine to dark mahogany. "It looks marvelous. What a stunning color. I knew it would look fantastic, but not this good."

"So, I have your approval?" He stood, a pleased smile on his face, and he put the trays on the kitchen countertop, making an area for her to leave her bag and the brushes.

"So, where are we eating lunch? The room is bare."

"On the floor. It's the cleanest surface in the place." He grabbed the sofa cushions from the hallway and tossed them onto the polished floor where they slithered to a halt. "Sit. I'll bring the sandwiches."

He had made nice cheese salad sandwiches, the chunky type that he took to work, and she enjoyed every bite. Tim had never made her a sandwich, or even a cup of tea, and having a lunch prepared for her was ridiculously pleasing. "The paint's in the trunk of my car," she said, after her last bite. "Am I cutting-in or rolling?"

"I think you ought to cut-in unless you don't like my ladder. It's nothing special."

"I'd rather because I think I'm good with a brush. Do you have a few groundsheets? I'd hate to mess up your lovely floor."

He had left a few old bed sheets on a chair in the hallway, and he skidded them across the polished floor in her direction. "I'll get the paint."

"You'll need me, too, because you won't be able to carry all the cans alone."

He gave her a look of patient incredulity but she went outside anyway. She had taken three trips to the car with her three cans and she would rather help him carry; then she could get him to help spread the sheets.

Two accomplished far more than one and within five minutes, the floor mainly covered, she stood on the third top rung of his ladder, cutting the green into the cornices. She painted fast, but he easily kept up with the roller.

When the first coat covered the first wall, she climbed down the ladder and stood back, eyes narrowed, assessing the job. "What do you think?"

"Are we using beige on the other walls?"

She took a breath. "I made an executive decision. That blue-green looked deadly with beige but gorgeous with the color I mixed. I discovered a green pale enough to be just off white and I added yellow." She put down her brush, found the lid opener on the kitchen countertop with the spare roller trays, and revealed the paint.

He didn't say a word about the color, but he smiled. He had the sort of smile that conveyed unspoken messages, this one a sign of approval. "So, we'll do the other three with this. Do you want to swap jobs?"

"Do you?"

"Nope. Lead on."

And within another hour or so, they had finished all four walls, though the kitchen area was simply a small strip above the top cupboards. Nevertheless, her arms ached and the arches of her feet wanted to cramp from standing on the narrow rung for so long. She stepped down, relieved. She'd looked over the walls while she was painting, of course, but judging from the color combination, the very pale citrus and the medium bluish green, she expected to love the room. "Oh. My…"

"…gosh," JD said in a dry tone, standing back with her. "It looks good. You have an interesting take on colors. You clearly have an excellent eye for this sort of thing."

"Or two. Thanks. Though, it kind of makes the ceiling look stale, though."

He sighed. "You could have given me two or three seconds before you mentioned that. We have to put another coat on each wall before we can do anything else. I think it's time for a break. Do you want tea or coffee?"

She sat on the floor, slid off her canvas shoes, and pulled her toes back, easing out the cramp. "Coffee, please. And an apple." The last request was pure cheek. She'd seen fruit in his fridge when he took the milk out.

He threw her an apple and took one himself so that her crunching melded with his. After he brought the coffee over, he sat on the floor with her, the mugs between them on the sheets. Without a sign of being uncomfortable, he took her foot into his big hands and massaged between bites of his apple. "You'll have apple flavored feet after this."

She giggled like an idiot. "I can't think of anything more wonderful than a foot massage at this moment."

"Give me the other foot. I can't have one of my workers disabled."

She dropped her gaze, guilty of enjoying his touch too much. This was a job, as he had reminded her, and not a social occasion. She took both feet back when he had eased the second and sat cross-legged, sipping her coffee, which reenergized her.

With barely a word of conversation unrelated to the job or the *High Society* set, she cut-in the ceiling, the sidewalls, the doorway, the window, and the skirting boards while he followed with the roller. She barely noticed they had almost ended the job until she saw she had reached the first green wall again.

Standing back, she watched him race his roller over the last single-coated citrus area. He looked as if he could paint for hours, his methodical strokes neatly swishing from top to bottom.

"And now the worst part," she said in a dire tone, glancing at him.

"The ceiling?"

She shook her head. "The cleaning up."

"I'll do it. You sit and contemplate your feet. I can see you are wanting to take your shoes off again."

"I need monkey toes for that sort of ladder."

"Aha. So, I'm on my own for the ceiling?"

"I didn't bring ceiling paint. Plus, I don't think I could manage any more painting today."

"I'm glad you said that. I've had enough, too. I'm buying takeaway for tonight's meal. What do you want?"

"Thanks, but I'll need to get home." She glanced at her watch. "It's almost six. It's getting dark outside."

"Two people can't paint a whole room in less than half a day," he said, his thumbs hooked into his front pockets and his eyebrows drawn together. "Well, not properly." He shrugged. "And I'm sorry that you want to leave. I was hoping we could spend a little time together…or do you have a date?"

She would have liked to say yes, but she couldn't when he was watching her expression so closely. A bad liar all her life, she told the truth, mainly. Looking away from him, she said, "I want a shower, a meal, and a rest, preferably in front of the TV."

"My thoughts, exactly." He rubbed his hands together like a stage villain, and he grinned not at all melodramatically but as if he was pleased. "So, what do you want to eat?"

"You're a user, you know that?" Faking outrage, she placed her hands on her hips. "You can't get takeaway without my car, can you?"

For a moment he looked puzzled, an expression lost in a blink. "You can have a shower while I go."

"And you'll be back sometime next week unless you borrow my car."

His mouth twisted into a half smile, and he shrugged. "I can take my bike."

She laughed. "Don't be so manipulative." Turning, she reached for her handbag on the kitchen countertop. "I would really love to have a shower before I eat takeaway. Just tell me you have a current driver's license, and you can take the car. I'll have chicken and a Greek salad."

"I have a driver's license." He stared at her.

She tossed him the keys.

He left, whistling.

* * * *

When Jay arrived back, although the floor was still covered, the table, with two chairs pulled up beneath, sat back near the countertop. Vix had set out knives and forks. Although he had never noticed before, he could smell his shower gel on her, and his mouth watered. She looked lovely with her hair combed into a soft, low bunch on her neck, and her makeup refreshed.

He dumped the foil-lined pack holding the chicken and the plastic containers of salad on the counter top. "Did you find the wine in the fridge?"

"I didn't open the fridge."

He blinked. Lonny would have been through his fridge, his CDs, and most of his drawings in the third bedroom if he left her alone in the house for any extended period. She regularly raided his bedroom for shirts, which she wore tied around her middle like Daisy Duke. Half-surprised that Vix hadn't helped herself to anything, but half-pleased, he grabbed the glasses and poured the wine, while she efficiently cut and served the chicken and salad.

He kept forgetting she'd been married and had likely served a meal most nights of those years. "I'm glad to see you got the green paint off your jeans."

"House paint." She clicked her tongue with mock disapproval. "It's not like scenic paint and easy to scrub off. While I was shifting the table back, I noticed you don't have a TV. You misled me." She took a sip of her wine. "I should have gone home for a shower and a meal."

"I have a TV. It's in the second bedroom at the moment. When we've finished eating, I'll shift the couch and the coffee table back and we'll be reasonably comfortable."

She insisted on helping him shift the couch, though he could have carried the two-seater on his own. The secret to keeping her in his house was to continue needing her help, and so he let her carry in the small coffee table while he carried in the television set. She finished her wine and he refilled her glass. His had hardly been touched.

She snuggled her bare feet beneath her on the couch as she settled with the TV program guide. "I can't believe I wanted to watch television. It's Saturday. There's nothing on TV that I would watch."

"Aren't you the fussy one? There are two perfectly good, constantly repeated movies on tonight. Take your pick."

She chose the fifth rerun of *I Am Sam*, which they'd both seen enough times to be able to talk through, easily and happily. He liked being with her. He enjoyed her conversation. She asked interesting questions, made intelligent comments, and she understood his sense of humor. Her presence stimulated him. Plus, she was gorgeous. He could look at her all day.

She had a straight nose, big gleaming eyes, and a mouth that fascinated him. When she smiled, her lips stretched half across her cheeks, and the corners of her mouth turned upward. Her teeth were such a pure white as to be almost transparent. No one seeing her smile couldn't be happy, and that smile made her pretty face into a stunning face. He wanted her to smile all the time.

Finally, the end credits rolled and she glanced at her watch. "Do you want me to help paint the ceiling tomorrow?"

"I don't think you could stand all that ladder-work."

"You should do the ladder-work. Those cornices are labor intensive and so is the ceiling-rose. They're probably '40s-made, but they have an art deco look. I could make my life easy and use an extension on the roller."

"Your help would be much appreciated. I wouldn't take on the ceiling alone, not tomorrow. I'm too out of shape." He slowly stretched one arm and then the other, and found he had her full attention.

"You don't look out of shape." She moistened her lips, glancing away from him. "Do you want to start early or later?"

"Early, I think. Then we'll have time to do something a bit more stimulating in the afternoon. I think you ought to stay tonight." He paused, noting an expression of surprise flit across her face. Meaning to keep his request casual, he said, "I don't see the need for you to keep travelling to and fro while we're working here. Do you?"

She made a thinking face, her lovely mouth slightly awry and her fingers pressing into her chin. "I don't have a toothbrush or clean underwear."

"I have a spare toothbrush or two and you can wash out your underwear. It will dry overnight."

"You have a spare room, you said." Her eyes questioned him.

He rubbed his jaw, hoping he looked dubious. "It's a mess. I've left all my books from this room on the bed, and some of the smaller furniture is still there. I can sleep on the couch if you're worried I'll make a move on you."

Her teeth caught the edge of her bottom lip and she looked away from him. "I could hardly worry that you might make a move on me. I gave you every opportunity a week ago, and you didn't."

"So, I can sleep in my own bed with you?"

"The guys know who you sleep with," she said in a careful voice, her forehead slightly creased.

He shook his head. "Not a chance. They don't know you were here the first time, and they won't know you are here tonight."

"I'm not talking about me. I'm talking about another, unnamed woman. Steve saw her on Wednesday morning and he assumes you are having a relationship with her. What would she think if she knew I spent the night?"

He shrugged. "What would Steve have thought if he saw her leaving last Sunday morning? The same thing, but you were here. You know Lonny only dropped in. She often does that. And she knows you spent the night, though she doesn't know who you are."

She wet her lips, clearly mulling over the information. Finally, she gave a long deep sigh. "I don't want to put myself in the position of being the other woman. You insist you are not having a relationship with her, and since you're not with her tonight and you weren't with her last Saturday night, or Sunday, and I know she dropped by on Sunday morning, I have to believe you. I also know I can sleep platonically with you. That couch is a two-seater. A man your size couldn't possibly spend the night there." She looked away. "I don't want to make this a big deal when it isn't, and if I sleep over we can get the ceiling done in no time. I'm really dying to see the sheets off the floor, and the whole picture. The reveal. The part I love best about sets is when the curtain rises and I can see the first visual of the story."

"So, that means you're staying over?"

She nodded. "And this time I want hot milk in bed, not cold." She poked his chest and sounded rich and spoiled. Then she laughed, ruining the whole effect. "Although I would have liked you to be attracted to me, it's much better this way. I can stay over without feeling awkward."

Which, of course, put him out no end. If he had said he was attracted to her, she wouldn't assume she could sleep with him platonically. He'd had no intention of being her guy-pal. He was Lonny's guy-pal. He wanted Vix. He wanted her arms and legs around him, her mouth on his, and he wanted to hear her sighs. He wanted to comb his fingers through her soft, shiny hair, and he wanted to clench a bunch while he kissed her as he thrust inside her.

Okay, he wanted her to feel relaxed with him as well, but that was purely because the sex would be better if she wasn't defensive, as she had been on the first night, defensive, scared, and assuming she could use him. Possibly another man wouldn't mind being used that way, but for him, sex needed to be more than simply physical exercise.

Relaxing his shoulders and trying for a casual tone, he said, "And to make sure neither of us feels awkward in the morning, I'm pulling the couch over to block the kitchen door. I don't want another early morning visitor."

"Why does she have a key to your house?"

"She lived here for a while after her last relationship blew up. I didn't ask for the key back because it didn't matter then. It does now, and I'll get it back." He smiled at her, pleased to see she didn't look at all distrustful nor even slightly suspicious of his motive in getting her to stay the night, not that he really had a motive. He simply had a hope that sleeping with him in his bed would keep her comfortable around him. Relaxed and enjoyable sex would follow on from that. "I assume you'll want something to wear to bed, since your underwear will be elsewhere." He sucked in a breath, wishing he didn't know that.

"I'm not wearing any frilly negligee of yours," she said with mock affront. "I'm more of a T-shirt girl."

He grinned. "I can manage a T-shirt." Under the guise of assessing her size, he assessed her shapely body, hoping he looked nothing but platonic. He felt anything but platonic, and he had to leave to disguise the fact that his "um" would likely betray the truth.

After rummaging in a bedroom drawer for a while, he found an old and very big black T-shirt with a motorbike on the front. He offered this, and he left the bedroom and bathroom to her while he returned the TV and coffee table to the hallway and shifted the couch in front of the back door. Finally, he heard her leave the bathroom and enter his bedroom. By the time he got there, too, teeth cleaned and with condoms aplenty, she was lying on the far side of the bed, her hair loose over the pillow, the sheet pulled up to her chin, and clearly fast asleep.

He rubbed the back of his neck, sighing. He had let her work too hard during the day. Now he had his just desserts. She was exhausted. Dressed in his pajama shorts, he climbed into bed, too.

Chapter 8

Vix threshed, half-asleep, half-awake, and wholly aroused. She rolled from her back to her side, squeezing her thighs together to contain the sexual heightening that had only ever happened in her sleep. The intense excitement would end if she fully awoke, leaving her throbbing and unfulfilled. Her eyelids tightened and her hand grasped between her legs, gripping, letting go, not knowing what to do to ease her frustration. Her head whipped from side to side and she moaned softly, needing an end, wanting the culmination of the orgasm that never came.

When she rolled against JD's knee, she snapped into awareness. She pressed her lips together, closed her throat, and stopped squirming, but he straightened his leg and pulled her into his big comforting body. His solid chest molded to her back and his hand spanned her belly. She covered his fingers with hers, hoping he wouldn't wake up, but the waves of pleasure kept her rocking, kept her thighs tight, her mouth shut, and her aching need foremost.

With a sleepy mutter, JD tilted her hip back so that she half lay on top of him. Only the cotton of his sleeping shorts separated them. She moved her palm backwards to the skin of his hard, muscled thigh to reassure him, and he settled his lips in the juncture of her neck and shoulder while moving slightly away. For a moment, she dropped flat before, with one arm, he turned her belly to belly with him.

His eyes were shut and he breathed steadily. The man was clearly sleep-cuddling. Her noises hadn't woken him, nor had her thrashing around. Fortunately, she was fully awake now and easing down from her desperate peak. Between her legs, the throb turned into a mere tingle. She would sleep again soon, too, or she might have had he not given a twist of his hips. She almost gasped. His erection pressed into her from her pubis to her waist.

She contained herself. At no stage had his regular breathing pattern changed. He still drew in breath like a man asleep. She wished she could take advantage of him, open her legs, and rub herself against that beautiful hard tool of his, but surely that would be unethical. And so she lay against him, trying to pretend she was asleep, too. Deciding to retreat slowly, she eased back her top leg.

His hand caught her knee, which he placed over his hip and held. He moved right into her and his penis, dick, whatever he called the thing, pressed lengthwise between her legs. The pleasure was so intense that she shuddered.

"JD," she said, barely above a whisper. "Are you awake?"

He made a low sound like a laugh. "You'd better believe it."

"Do you know what you are doing to me?"

"Nothing…yet."

"You're teasing me." Tim had never leaned into her with an erection. His male body part had shriveled when she came near and he needed her hand to build him to pleasure, or her mouth, and if she made the slightest wrong move, he shriveled again. "You're making me…ache." With her ineptness, she had driven Tim to another woman, a sexy, beautiful woman. Vix had also turned JD off last week by wanting to have sex with him. "It's not fair."

He took a short breath. "How do you expect a man to sleep when you sound as if you want him—feel as if you want him?"

"I do." Her pulses jumped and shifted into her chest. "Want you."

Very slowly, he put a hand on the nape of her neck and combed his fingers up though her hair, setting the mass on top of her head. "So, will you let me give you pleasure?" He breathed against her throat.

"You are giving me pleasure."

"So, let's get you naked and more pleasured." He kissed below her ear again, and then grasped the hem of the T-shirt she wore.

She was fit and slim now and not ashamed of her figure. However, her self-consciousness stayed his hand for a moment. He couldn't see her, she knew, and he probably wouldn't tell her if she didn't look good. Taking in a tentative breath, she relaxed her grip, and he lifted the T-shirt over her head. Surreptitiously naked and trying to wear her skin with confidence, she pushed at him, sat up, and flicked the cover to the end of the bed.

He hadn't slept bare as the other woman had said, and so, thudding with apprehension, she leaned over him and put her hands under the elastic waistband of his shorts.

He half turned, and lifted to one elbow. "Not so fast."

Her mouth dried and the previous scenario flashed through her mind. He would kiss her, keep teasing her; then he would decide that they both needed a glass of milk. She knew that if he only played with her expectations this time, she would give up completely. "If I'm bare, the least you could do is take off those shorts."

He flipped off his shorts, and she wished he slept with the blind up. She wanted to see the whole of his naked body. Already she knew the dressed detail, the wide shoulders, the muscular arms, the lean hips, the tight buttocks, and his long legs. Her eyes had adjusted slightly to the dark and she could see his outline but not a lot of detail. She wanted to touch him to find out if he was still erect, but if she did and he had shriveled, she wouldn't proceed. She didn't want to take him into her mouth and pretend. Her sexual excitement waned and she turned onto her back, her wrist over her hot, prickling eyes.

He leaned onto one elbow and combed his fingers through her hair again, lifting the bulk high and to the side of the pillow. Then, he bent over her and kissed her just below her jaw. His breath was hot and his naked upper body brushed her breasts. Her nipples tightened and her heart began to thunder again.

She spread one tentative palm across his wide back, daring to hope but not daring to make a single wrong move. His lips began to explore every part of her face, from her chin, to her cheeks, to her forehead, to each of her eyes, and finally to her mouth, which he kissed lightly but thoroughly. He ran a hand down the side of her body beneath her buttocks, which he lifted under him as he shifted over her.

She lay beneath him, the dampness between her legs embarrassing, while he ran slow kisses over her neck and face. She arched into him. Surely this time he would penetrate her. He'd widened her legs and let the bulk of his hardness press into her belly. Sliding her hands from the bunching muscles of his bottom to the flatness of his abdomen, she edged her fingers around his penis.

He stopped her. Reaching under his pillow, he fumbled.

"What?" she asked, breathless.

"A condom." He took the pack to his mouth, flicked his head, and tore across with his teeth. She saw the plastic flutter against his breath. Rising to his knees, he took the ring of latex out of the pack, which he blew away while he rolled the condom on.

"You're so good at that," she said, now knowing for certain that last time he had deliberately ripped the condom, "you can even do it one-handed."

"Call it motivation." Lifting over her, he supported his weight on his straight arms while he kept the pressure of his hips against her. His penis searched, parted her, and teased in her moisture. Desperately excited, she clutched his buttocks. He dropped the length of his body on her and rolled them both to one side. She clenched her teeth, making a sound of utter frustration.

His mouth took hers in a long slow kiss, and when her neck relaxed, his palm opened over her breast. She moved his hand away. Continuing the kiss, he traced his fingers along the skin under her arm on the way to his former object, her breast. She squeezed his fingers and moved them to her hip. "I don't like having my breasts touched," she muttered against his mouth.

He kissed her bottom lip while his uppermost hand passed between their bodies, tracking a path down her abdomen to the area between her legs. She held her breath, hoping he wouldn't try to touch her, but he sought her moisture with his fingers. "No. Please. That hurts."

"What, this?" He touched her in the same susceptible place that made her nervy. She straightened her leg, denying him access. "Why does it hurt?

"I'm sensitive there."

"You're supposed to be sensitive there."

"Do I have to be like every other girl you've—screwed?"

"No." He shifted his hand to her hipbone.

"You don't have to prepare me. I'm ready. I've been ready for a week, and I want you to get it over with. I can't bear this, being with the sexiest man I've ever met, and being teased."

"I'm sexy?" he said, cupping her buttocks. His lips searched her jaw, her chin, and her throat.

"You're big and hard and you smell good."

"You're funny and sweet and you have a body that a man wants to do more than imagine. I want to put my hands all over you."

Since he was still erect, she knew her body appealed to him and so she wriggled against him, hooked one leg over his thigh and pressed her heel into the back of his knee, lifting her pelvis forward. "Please, please," she whispered, cupping his face with her palms.

He blew out his breath and eased her onto her back again. She widened her legs and rested her feet flat on the bed. His buttocks tightened, beginning a slow forward angling of hips and a penetration inside. He hurt her as he entered her, and she tightly clutched his bottom, trying to relax. If the sexiest man she'd known couldn't give her enjoyment, no man could.

She could see his face, his stark pleasure. His eyes half-closed, and she could hear him breathe though his mouth. The rhythm built and her body reacted with a surge of moisture. And her pleasure began to build until suddenly he stopped moving.

"If you keep your hips still, I should be able to get you there before I finish."

She closed her eyes, breathing frantically, prepared to do anything he asked if she could just orgasm, just once not fail. The build-up, the anticipation had been everything she wanted and needed. Even the way his knees held hers apart excited her.

He pulled out a little. His weight lifted and one of his hands pressed on her mound. Then, his fingers glided into her moisture.

She opened her eyes. "No."

He froze. "Yes. It'll have to be now."

"Well, do it now." Pushing his hand away, she wound her legs firmly around him, urging him on with her hip movements.

"I don't know what the hell you're doing to me. Vix, don't you want—"

"I want you. Now." She closed her eyes, concentrating on her need. Her legs trembled and she arched her body. While he hesitated, she wanted to scream and tear at him. Her frustration had become a physical pain.

He made a short, sharp sound of acceptance, and began to move again. She needed him too much, and she urged him with her body until he plunged harder and deeper, his slamming force shifting her until her head touched the wooden bed head. She clung to him and he grasped her and she knew she was building to a peak.

He expanded inside her and stilled, breathing out. His heart pounded loud enough to hear. Nothing had happened. While she waited expectantly, he withdrew. She hadn't experienced anything other than excitement. The anticipated climax had been the usual anti-climax.

Disappointed, she turned her head away. The lurching of the bed told her he was disposing of the condom. She didn't glance at him. She didn't want to die, but she didn't particularly want to give a party at that moment either.

The bed dipped again as he moved to take her into his arms. She covered her chest with her elbows doubled to keep him away.

"Yeah, well," he said in a casual voice. "What did you expect? An orgasm?"

"Yes," she answered tersely.

"Vix," he said, his voice strained. "You said no."

"I couldn't have asked more clearly. I thought you were different. I thought you could do it."

"Not with my hands tied. Do you usually have vaginal orgasms?"

"You shouldn't ask women things like that."

"Look, I don't know anything about vaginal orgasms. I don't know if a woman is having one, or faking. I do know about clitoral orgasms, though I suppose they could be faked, too. I just want to know which is more likely in your experience."

"Neither. That's why I wanted you."

He rolled onto his back and put his palms beneath his head. "You wanted my dick. That's what I gave you. A vibrator would be just as efficient."

Prickling with inadequacy, she curled herself into a protective ball. "I didn't fail. It was you. I'm not frigid. I'm sure that when I find the right man…" She felt him shake his head.

"You won't have an orgasm without stimulation, not if you've never had one. Open your legs." He leaned over her, jerked her arms aside, and with his elbow pressed her knee flat on the bed.

She took her other leg over and curled away from him. With a sigh, he put a palm on each of her knees and eased them apart. Strangely enough, he didn't frighten her, but he did embarrass her. What she had between her legs hadn't been made to look at, and she couldn't understand why he wasn't repulsed.

He dipped his head and licked her. Had she been able, she would have jerked away, but with her knees splayed apart, she could do no more than wriggle. Her back was already pressed against the bed head.

"Okay. You've humiliated me enough," she said, trying to sound casual. "You've implied I'm a failure. I don't know that I need anything else."

"Since you don't know, I'll give you what I think you need." He lifted her legs over his shoulders and stayed where he was.

She leaned forward and grabbed his hair but his tongue flattened and soothed. Having his mouth caress her made her breath stop. Experiencing a sinful pleasure, instead of pulling his hair, she tangled her fingers into the soft shaggy mass. He lifted her buttocks and her legs relaxed. She made needy noise. Her knees fell to the crooks of his elbows. He angled his head slightly and the bristles on his chin rubbed her skin, but his tongue continued to soothe. Her head arched back farther. She knew she should stop him but every nerve center focused between her legs.

A nice girl shouldn't enjoy what this bad boy did, but she could either envy bad girls for the rest of her life or try for a lack of inhibition. Taking a shaky breath she attempted to relax, which now seemed easier. Her enjoyment intensified and without a conscious thought, she ran her hand over his hair and urged him on. Greed took over, and she swiveled her hips in an effort to gain maximum gratification, tightening her fingers against his scalp, not knowing what she wanted him to do, but so badly wanting him to continue that she made encouraging noises and tried to find a comfortable place against the bed head.

With a sound of frustrated desire, he dragged her down in the bed, taking her more deeply with his mouth. She watched, excited by seeing his head between her legs. Never before had she been so out of control, so frantic. His thumbs teased at her until her body began to jerk involuntarily. Her insides contracted and she felt a gush of intense lingering pleasure. She loosened her grip on his hair and fell back, gasping, satisfied, her fingertips barely touching his wide shoulders.

She knew she'd climaxed, but she didn't know what to do, what to say. "Thank you" seemed inadequate. His thumb caresses ceased. He seemed to be kissing her…down there, slowly, carefully, and tenderly.

His kiss surprised her, and her heart expanded in her chest. Not only was he the sexiest man in the world, he was incredibly skilled with his lovemaking, with helping a woman feel cherished, safe, and desirable. She only needed what he'd given her, the experience that had proven Tim wrong.

With a real man, she could be a real woman.

"It seems you knew what you were talking about."

"Practice makes perfect."

"Don't brag."

"I was meaning you should have more practice."

"Now?"

He took her hand to his monstrous erection. "I can go slower this time."

"No," she said, searching for the bed cover. "Thanks."

He stretched out beside her. "Jesus!" he said in a voice of frustration. "You don't make anything easy for a man."

She averted her eyes from his muscular frame. She appreciated the casual display of his erection and she loved touching the big beautiful thing but she'd had him and she'd had an orgasm. Any more and she would turn into a begging fool, and she didn't intend to humiliate herself ever again. She didn't answer him and he didn't say another word. He rolled over with his back to her.

* * * *

Vix awoke, stretching luxuriously, and opened her eyes. The blind had been pulled up and the bright morning light streamed in, highlighting the tired lilac-gray walls and the bare wooden floor. Water ticked through the pipes outside and pattered like rain into the bath next door. Alone, she smiled, happy, content, a satisfied woman at last, pleased to have woken up alone. She didn't know how JD's mood would be this morning, but he was a big boy and he had to learn to cope with rejection. She had, for years.

Practicing an oblivious smile, she planned to shower as soon as he finished in the bathroom. Then, she would dress again in her painting clothes, ready to help with the ceiling. This would be how to act, as if last night had never happened—just a smile and straight back to being JD's painter. She found the black T-shirt on the floor and pulled the worn fabric over her head.

The flow of the water stopped and she barely had time to sit up, take her knees to her chin, and tug the T-shirt down to her ankles before JD entered, wrapped in a towel from the waist down. His hair had been slicked back, accenting his wonderful facial structure.

"Sleep well?" he asked, sounding grumpy.

She gave him her best casual smile and rested her cheek on her knee. "I recall a slight disturbance in the middle of the night. I'm not certain I remember…"

He shook his head, his face relaxing. "I can remind you from time to time."

She dropped her gaze, knowing she had to keep up her guard. "I need a shower."

"We slept late. I normally cook breakfast on Sundays, but if you are going to shower, I'll buy the ceiling paint and cook when I get back."

"Perhaps I could cook. Would you mind?"

"Not at all." He turned his back, opening his wardrobe door. "I have eggs and bacon, sausages if you like, and bread in the fridge. The hardware shop is a couple of blocks away so I'll take the bike." He dropped his towel.

His back view was stunning, the wide muscled shoulders, the narrow waist and the hard, hard buttocks, a glorious handful each. She breathed through her mouth, knowing she should leave for the bathroom.

"Take the car. You'll need a couple of cans, at least. My keys are in the kitchen."

He slipped on a pair of blue jocks and then his jeans. "Then I'll be even faster," he said, turning. "Get a move on, woman. We don't have all day." He smiled, reluctantly.

She scooted off the bed, grabbing at her jeans and top. "Breakfast will be ready to go as soon as you arrive back."

Within fifteen minutes, she was fresh and clean, her wet hair knotted back and her makeup lightly applied. She noted that JD had moved the sofa away from the back door, and so she set the table, put the kettle on to boil, and took the bacon and eggs out of the fridge. A shadow passed the back window. Waiting, she looked up. She hadn't heard the car arrive back.

The back door opened and the shapely female figure in the doorway paused, staring at the paint spattered sheets covering the floor. "JD," she called in a surprised voice, and she must have noticed Vix's startled move in the kitchen. "Oh." The woman stood, her face a question.

"I'm Vix." Vix cleared her dry throat. "JD will be back any moment. He went to buy the paint for the ceiling," she said far too fast, far too awkwardly, and in a slightly panicked tone, not knowing if she'd been left in a difficult situation or just an embarrassing one.

The woman who confronted her was every man's dream, medium height and slim. Her white-blond hair had been casually draped over one shoulder along with a large Italian leather bag patterned in blue and gray zigzags. She proudly displayed her noteworthy cleavage in a short, tight blue top. Her long, slender legs were also on show beneath her abbreviated denim shorts, which she had zipped but not buttoned over her tanned belly. Her mouth pursed as she assessed Vix, flitting over her hair. "You would be the painter of the set he is currently working on."

"Yes," Vix said, relieved to be given a reason to be in JD's house in the morning. "I'm helping him paint the room. And, ah, I was invited for breakfast. You must be Lonny."

Lonny nodded. "Typical JD. He left you to cook. He loves to act like a helpless male but a less helpless male I've yet to meet. He's actually quite a good cook. Better than me." She bent her head forward, flicked her hair, rearranging her locks back into the same place. "And he told me you're a better painter than I am. Since he said he'd rather have an expert, I won't stay."

"Did you come to paint?" Vix blinked with ridiculous disappointment. She'd assumed JD needed her. "He won't be long. He's only at the hardware shop."

Lonny pressed a finger to her mouth while she considered. "I'm thinking he meant to surprise me with the new room and I don't want to ruin his pleasure. Please don't tell him I dropped by." She smiled. "Nice to finally meet you, Vix. Give my regards to the team." The door closed behind her.

For a moment, Vix stayed staring at the door. Since her car wasn't in the driveway, Lonny had expected JD to be alone. However, she knew more about Vix than Vix knew about her. JD had clearly discussed her. Vix found she didn't like being talked about with another woman. She turned back to the kitchen with half a mind not to cook breakfast. That would teach him...nothing. They didn't have a relationship. They'd actually just had the one-night stand she'd tried for last week.

Firming her mouth and her shoulders, she whipped the eggs into a frenzy and then sat and waited for him to return.

Chapter 9

Jay grabbed a can of white ceiling paint and proceeded to the busy checkout to pay. Sunday at the Port Adelaide shopping center was as busy as any other day, and he had to wait while people asked the sales attendants basic questions like "What sort of screw do I need for..." He thrummed his fingers on his can, planning how to reimburse Vix for the rollers and paintbrushes she had bought. Cash might be awkward. He doubted she would stand around while he counted out spare change into her palm. Perhaps he could pay her in kind, that was, buy her dinner.

But where? She would have been everywhere he couldn't afford. Brought up by her blue-blooded father, James Tremain, she would always have had the best of everything money could buy. The man was no miser. He had, in fact, supported Jay for four years of his life by extending the university scholarship, originally endowed by him for a two-year master's degree, from the first year to the fifth. This gave Jay the opportunity to be an architect, which for the son of a drunk had always been an impossible dream. His father spent every cent of his dole money on alcohol. At times he had even stolen money from his sons when they had been careless enough to leave cash around. So, Jay had always known he had to earn money to support his younger brothers. After he matriculated, along with Steve and Trent, he accepted being apprenticed to a builder.

Later that year, his father died of liver failure. The Dee boys found themselves in possession of a shabby house piled high with empty bottles and bills. After Kell matriculated, like Jay he took on an apprenticeship, too. Jay hoped Luke would also finish high school if he could keep off Sherry long enough. For a couple of years, a rookie builder and an apprentice cabinetmaker supported three large, hungry males. Then Luke finished his plumbing apprenticeship and married Sherry. Jay and Kell decided to use their wages to set Luke up in his own business since he had a child to support within six months of marriage.

Had it not been for Jay's former principal, Jay might have been a tradesman for the rest of his life, but Mr. Trevor decided to interfere because of Jay's extraordinary matriculation results. He couldn't bear the waste, he had said, and he wrote a detailed letter to James Tremain, known for his altruism. Although prickling with the humiliation of being a worthy cause, Jay completed a portfolio and was accepted into the university with a full scholarship, which included a living allowance.

His first year was dominated by charismatic Tim Nolan, an architect idolized by his students. Tim's wit and charm wore thin with Jay before his second year, after he found out how a fellow female student had inexplicably managed to top his grades. He didn't have much time for Tim after that and kept out of his way, but no one could have failed to know when Tim married the very rich and very young Victoria Tremain. Tim managed to feature in the celebrity pages constantly, often pictured with the wife whose earlier photos showed a pretty young woman with a dazzling smile and whose later photos hinted at a woman who had decided to let her husband take the limelight.

In Jay's third year of university, during which he worked for his bachelor degree, he took Lonny as his date to an end-of-year function attended by his fellow students and lecturers. By then, she had made a nominal success of her hairdressing business by employing makeup artists and stylists. After attracting a famous client, she had greatly expanded her list, and the social pages in the daily newspaper mentioned her at least once a week, sometimes more, often publishing photos of her with celebrities.

In a sideways move at the function, she hooked up with Tim Nolan. Tim assumed he had won her from Jay, and made enough smarmy comments to earn Jay's loathing. Lonny assumed he was jealous, which made anything he said against Tim sound like sour grapes. Unwilling to set himself up as a moral watchdog, he kept his opinions to himself when she dropped by. None knew better than he how much she needed a friend, despite her doing her best to discard everyone she had known in the old days. At the end of his fourth year, he saw Ilona and Tim in a nightclub. He saw Tim slap Ilona. The rest was history.

Tremain had been disappointed to hear that the recipient of his generosity had been convicted of assaulting his son-in-law. No doubt the little flea in his ear, Tim the Tom, had embellished the story to get Tremain to rescind his largesse.

If Tremain knew an untrustworthy, ungrateful felon was now messing with his lovely daughter, he would be appalled. Jay didn't think the right word was messing, nor anything cruder. Captivated—or involved—would be a better word. He swung the can onto the front seat of Vix's dinky little red car and drove home through the crammed pot-holed streets.

A woman with Vix's assets wouldn't consider him as a life-partner, but last night had him plotting how to get her to stay around for a while. His draw-card was that she enjoyed sex but she didn't seem to think she should be participating in the best recreational activity known to man or woman. She might be emotionally detached from him now, but if could keep her interested with good sex, she just might see that she liked him.

He strode through the back door, spotting Vix sitting at the kitchen table. She arose with a strange look on her face. "Breakfast will be ready in five minutes," she said, turning her back. She busied herself while he dried off yesterday's rollers and brushes at the outside sink.

Within five minutes, she called him inside and he sat down to a plate of fluffy scrambled eggs, bacon, and triangles of toast.

"Cute," he said, waving a piece, but her face said be grateful and he knew he was. In the real world, he wouldn't be sitting at breakfast with a talented, intelligent, well-connected woman like her. He needed to appreciate each moment that had no chance of lasting.

Like a team, they got on with painting the ceiling, him doing the brushwork on the art deco cornices and the elaborate ceiling centers. Only last year he had knocked down the wall between the two small rooms, joining them into one, opening out the space. And yes, he would open up the room more with a set of French doors, as Vix had suggested.

"How did you meet your husband?" he asked her, automatically moving his brush along the cornice.

"He knew my father."

"How old were you when you married?" he asked, although he knew. When they broke up, that information had been in the paper along with an old photo of Vix and her dazzling smile. And two-timing Tim.

"Twenty."

"Did your father mind you marrying so young?"

"Yes, but he couldn't stop me. He very graciously didn't say 'I told you so' when we divorced. He's a good man, my father. He brought me up alone for ten years after my mother died."

"So, he married again?"

"I have a six-year-old half-brother. He started school last year and he thinks he is very grown up now."

"Do you mind being supplanted?"

"No. It takes the pressure off. You would know that, having two siblings."

He nodded. His father had had three boys to knock around instead of one, which took the pressure off, slightly.

After finishing the complicated ceiling decoration in the middle of the sitting room, he moved the ladder to the kitchen to paint the second.

"How long have you known Steve and Trent?" she asked from the other side of the room, swishing the roller along her part of the ceiling.

"Twenty years. More, maybe. We were brought up in this neighborhood and went to the local school."

"Lonny went to the same school, too?"

"Yup." He took a filled liter can of paint up the ladder with him.

Vix had the big can to top up her roller tray. She was rolling paint fast. "And she's beautiful."

"Who, Lonny? Well, she knows how to present herself."

Vix glanced over at him. "Most of us can't tell the difference between beauty and presentation."

"Sure we can. Beauty is something extra. It's a smile, a way of moving, thinking…" He shook his head, not clear in his mind why Vix was beautiful and Lonny was great looking. "Who told you she is beautiful? Steve?"

"Probably. When you've done that and the cornices over the cupboards, we'll be finished, the first coat at least. Not a bad morning's work." She wiped her paint-spattered hands on the rag near her paint tray.

He finished off the central decoration and moved his ladder again. "How's the crick in your neck?"

She smiled. "Not as bad as yours, I'd say. Do you think we'll get away with just one coat—since it's white on white?"

He assessed the job over in her area where the painting had been finished. "We'll know when it's dry but it looks good. I'll be another five minutes."

She put her roller in a plastic bag while he completed the last cornice. When he had stepped down from his ladder, he saw she had pretty well tidied up. "You're amazing."

She gave him a look of surprise. "I'm a painter. That's what I do."

"I've worked with painters in various capacities for more than ten years and most are good, but not amazing. You've got what's known as a work ethic. I'm not paying you, but you work fast and you clean up as you go. I'm betting that your paintbrushes are as spotless as your rollers. And your work, although you're basically an artist, is as good as any housepainter. Plus, you smell better," he added casually as he moved towards her, his wet paintbrush in his hand. He put his other hand on her hip and leaned down, kissing the tip of her nose. "I'm beginning to think I buy sissy shower gel."

She laughed. "I had perfume in my bag. It's not your shower gel."

"Whew. I was just starting to wonder what the guys have been saying about me behind my back. Stay there. I've got a full paintbrush in my hand and any sudden move of yours might startle me." He gave her another kiss, this time on the lips. "I wouldn't want to get paint on that nice top of yours." With her attitude to sex, wanting to get the whole thing over and done with without much touching, he had the idea she'd missed out on romance, which he hoped to supply.

"I'm sure I've got a spot or two." Her eyes gleamed at her joke, because her top was red with little white dots.

"Stay. I've got another kiss to spare." He planted his next hopeful offering on her mouth, slightly opening her lips with the pressure of his. His other hand covered her behind and lifted her slightly into his growing erection.

She liked that; he could tell by the glaze of her eyes, but teasing her was more beneficial to his chance of a relationship than sex at this stage. "Coffee?"

Her hands had relaxed on his shoulders and she stiffened her arms and pushed him away, frowning. "Clearly, kissing reminds you that you need something to drink. At least it's not milk this time. Yes, coffee while we consider the next coat."

She looked disgruntled, which he enjoyed, but he hesitated for a moment. He couldn't be in love with a woman he'd met a week ago. He was merely fascinated by her and getting a little too involved in her thought processes, a little too charmed by her naturalness, and far too interested in sex with her.

In the end, when the paint had dried, the consensus of opinion was the one coat was enough. He made sandwiches.

* * * *

Vix should have left when the painting was finished, but since she'd met Lonny, she had seen Jay differently. He was an interesting attractive man, one that another woman had tried to warn Vix off. Vix had never thought she was competitive but she had no intention of leaving the field clear for Lonny. If Jay wanted the other woman, he was free to have her. Since his kisses this morning showed he wasn't willing to give up on Vix so easily, she could only be flattered by the whole scenario.

Plus, being human, she couldn't pass up a sandwich filled with cold takeaway chicken. While Jay took his ladder outside, she folded the sheets covering the glorious new floor which she hadn't seen since she had first arrived a little over twenty-four hours ago.

She stood back, waiting for Jay to walk in, which he did, examining the gleaming floor. "I don't think we marked it."

"Let's not be modest. Let's look at the walls and the floor and do some crass admiring."

He grinned. She liked the way he accepted her phrasing. Tim said she spoke like an adolescent, using superlatives when she could have been a little more sophisticated. Lonny would be more sophisticated. She was Tim's type and she would say the room looked very nice.

Vix said, "The room looks so stunning I can hardly breathe. It's cool and calm and the contrast of the floor with the walls is fantastic."

Jay nodded. "As I said, you're amazing. No one else would have helped me do this. No one else would have mixed the perfect colors, and I'm almost sure no one else would have persuaded me to strip the floor this year."

She put her hands on her hips. "I didn't say a word about stripping the floor."

"In a roundabout way, you did. You told me it would look wonderful and it does. What about the kitchen cabinets?"

She glanced over at the kitchen area. "They're cream."

"And?"

"Maybe they should be dark."

"My thought, exactly." He knocked knuckles with her, grinning. "I have some old floorboards I bought at auction that would make perfect door fronts. What do you think about white marble bench tops?"

"Too expensive for this house. Granite would be better."

"I think I'm in love with you."

She glanced at him, breathless for a moment. "Figuratively speaking."

"Of course." He gave a surprised smile. "We share the same taste. Want to help me move the furniture back?"

"It's going to be sacrilege, putting those old discards in this room."

The table and chairs, painted gray, already sat in place, as did the sofa. Next, she helped him carry back the huge wardrobe that had previously occupied the far end of the sitting room. This was old cedar and actually looked really good with the floor and was fortunately not too heavy because of the lack of insides. This he rectified by replacing various shelves, which made the cedar simply a decorative outside for a very clever, hidden, traditional sound system. "Did you make this?"

"Sure. It was a part of my greater plan." He said this with such a macho expression that she laughed, bringing back his mischievous grin. "It looks neater than open shelves."

Next, she helped him move the ghastly floral couch into position. Placed, the two-seater looked untidy. The loose cover was hitched up on one corner. To smooth the material, she hauled at the bottom frill. "You have a brown upholstery under here. If it's not too worn, it would look considerably better than faded blue flowers."

He nodded. "I left the floral as a dust cover. Do we want it off now?"

"It's your couch."

"So, I'll take it off." He passed her the cushions to unzip as he pulled up the main fabric. The last flip off the arm of the couch caused something to fly past his head and make a tinkling noise on the floor.

Vix swooped on a long silver earring, which she passed to him. "You must have been missing this." She unzipped the cushions and set them back on the couch, noting he put the earring in his pocket.

The room looked stunning now. The warmth of the dark floor, the cool crispness of the walls and the brown of the couch combined to make the whole place look fresh and smart. "So, let's bring in the blue coffee table and the gray armchairs," she said with a reluctant sigh.

"The coffee table is pine and not worth stripping. What color do you think I should paint it?"

"Ignore it, at this stage. You've got the couch and the wardrobe as your main pieces. If you are serious about stripping you could refinish the dining table and the chairs…Actually, I did a course in upholstery. I thought it would be useful as a set designer."

"Vix, are you offering to reupholster those two chairs?" He stared at her, his eyebrows lifted with surprise.

"I'm offering, but you have to strip them of gray paint first."

"I know you're not into stripping." He half-closed his eyes and scrutinized her face. One side of his mouth lifted. "But you like watching other people strip, don't you?"

She stared at her palm. "You're right. I certainly like watching you strip. You have a truly great body."

"Let's not sidetrack me. You have a truly great body, too, but you don't seem to think you have. We need to talk about last night. We got all this backward. I'd hardly kissed you when you headed for the bedroom on the night we met."

She pulled in her chin. "You knew my intentions were dishonorable. We discussed that."

"And then yesterday—just a kiss or two and we were in bed again with pretty well no foreplay. Then we had sex. Next, a bit of foreplay. To my way of thinking, I'm owed quite a bit of kissing. But first, I want to go out on a date with you. That's the way we should have started." He rubbed the back of his neck.

"Perhaps, if we were plotting a relationship—"

"I'm not all that interested in gratuitous sex. If we're going to end up in bed together, I'd like a relationship first."

She raised her chin, her insides tickling. "Well, there's a fine bit of blackmail."

"No relationship, no sex," he said, shoving his hands in his front pockets and staring at her. "I want a dinner date with you."

She shrugged. "So, that means you want sex with me. Why not skip the preliminaries?"

"I'm not that kind of guy."

She saw his mouth twitch. Either he or she would laugh first and she thought it ought to be him. So, she sighed, loudly. "You strike a tough bargain. Do you have date rules, too?"

"You'll need to pick me up. No flowers. We've gone too far for that."

She crossed her arms. "Do I have to book the restaurant and pay?"

"Try it," he said in a growly voice, "and you'll have to wait for the next date before you'll even get a kiss."

"I'm glad I checked. I could so easily have gotten this whole thing wrong." She walked over to her handbag on the kitchen countertop, checked her car keys, and gathered up both. "Wednesday. I'll pick you up at seven." With a swing of her hips, she strolled past him to the back door.

He passed her and opened it, walked her to her car, opened the driver's door and waited for her to step by him to get in. Before she did so, he swung her into his arms and gave her a thorough, far too sexy kiss. A little shaky, she started the car and drove off.

And then she laughed all the way to the main road. Romance wasn't for her, nor was getting too serious, but the guy had a certain male charm. She'd had an interesting two days without once feeling guilty about doing exactly as she pleased, helping, painting, talking idly, and flirting. For the first time in however long, she'd been involved in light-hearted banter and she'd had fun. Mentally, she connected with JD.

Sexually, well, since she needed experience, she wanted to experiment with him. He didn't put her down, he didn't make her feel ugly and awkward, and he didn't make her do anything she didn't want to do.

She'd had plenty of time to think about Lonny's visit early this morning. She'd had plenty of time to realize that Lonny had noted Vix's wet hair, and had added one and one. Just a friend who had heard about another woman would surely be pleased to meet her and certainly not so determined to put her in her place.

The room was being revitalized as a surprise for Lonny? That was actually an awful thing to say when Lonny clearly suspected Vix had slept with JD the night before. That would mean Lonny and JD had colluded to use Vix. Vix couldn't believe that of JD, a man who was loved by his family and respected by his coworkers.

So, for the first time in her life, a true-blue pin-up blonde tried to warn Vix off a man. How confidence bolstering was that?

* * * *

The next morning, Jay closed his front door at the same time Steve pulled up his car outside. As usual, Trent sat in the front and so Jay piled into the back.

"You won't believe it." Trent turned in his seat and blotted a fake yawn with his fist. "Guess who Steve hooked up with on Saturday night."

"Elton John."

"Very funny," Steve said, sounding cheerful. "Try guessing a female."

"k. d. lang."

Steve pulled the car into the peak-hour traffic. "You know, don't you, that's why you're not guessing?"

Trent smirked. "Ilona."

"Marge Simpson. No, too sensible for Steve. Snow White, too busy—"

"C'mon, JD." Steve switched off the car radio. "It was Lonny. There I was, sitting at the bar in the Dockside and guess who pulls up a stool beside me?"

"A stool? Ah, Little Miss Muffet."

"And she asks me if I want to go somewhere to eat," Steve said in an overdone mysterious tone.

"And the rest is X-rated, I presume?"

Jay saw Steve's shoulders rise in a shrug. "Yeah. We had a meal first. It was good. Not the meal, but the meal was okay. We had a steak in Semaphore. It was good going out with Lonny, is all."

"Play it cool, Steve. Don't seem so pleased to see her," Jay said in a serious voice. "Ask her out again and take her somewhere nice. She likes dressing up."

"I told her I'd ring her. She didn't say not to."

"You're in with a chance. Don't blow it."

"Do you reckon he's got a chance with Ilona?" Trent asked, turning to look at Jay.

"I think it's time she settled down. But with Steve?" Jay took his time considering, fingering his chin, mainly because Steve was watching him in the rear view mirror. "Maybe. Steve might be man enough to tame her." Given a challenge, Steve might measure up. If he did, great. Jay wanted everyone to be happy. He was. He stretched his aching shoulders. Painting ceilings was hell on necks.

During the day, he didn't need to hang around Vix. Seeing her was enough. He could watch her work, note her interest in doing every single thing from cutting stencils, marking off flats, making artificial leaves for the outdoors scenes, and mixing colors for special effects, like her marble pool edges. She faked the best marble he had ever seen because she made the finish subtle. She scraped on wood grain so well that he could swear he'd found an antique walnut table waiting around to be polished. Her job seemed to be more like an interesting pastime than work to her.

Within a month or two, his life would be like that. He would be doing a job he wanted to do, designing commercial buildings. Not at first. First, he'd be drafting, but he would work his way up the ladder. During the past few weeks, he had lined up a few interviews but he wanted to see the results of a competition he had entered before he began touting his wares.

Almost time for a lunch break, he used the sink in the cleanup area to wash his hands. From the other side of the barrier, he heard Vix's voice in the tearoom. "What's JD's name?"

"Jay Dee," Steve said, sounding puzzled.

"I mean his real name."

"Jay Dee."

"What's his surname, then?"

"Dee."

"So, his name is j-a-y, d-e-e? Why don't you call him Jay?"

"We've always called him JD. It's kind of a joke."

Jay stepped into the room. "My father's name was Hugo. My mother's name was Isla. HD, ID, and so they thought the first child should be JD. So they called me Jay. And because most people think Jay Dee is my nickname, they call me Jay Dee. If Kell had been a girl, he would have been Kay. Even I can't imagine what Luke might have been."

Vix wrinkled her forehead, concentrating. "He's the father of M, N, and O, Max, Noah, and Oscar. I'm guessing there's a real competition between you and Kellen to produce P and Q," Vix said, her hands on her hips, her face a picture of amusement.

Jay laughed. "He can go first. I'd like to see him with a son called Quigly."

"Quentin," Steve said with a grin.

"Are we doing this one again?" Trent asked as he walked into the tearoom. "Quin."

"Quincy." Kell punched the air behind him. "It's a race to the bottom that I'll leave Jay to win."

"Quockadile," Vix said and Jay had to leave the room.

He thought he might bust a gasket laughing. Not another woman in the world would have said something so seriously nerdy to a pack of guys.

He was definitely in love.

Chapter 10

On Wednesday night, Vix finally had the chance to dress up for Jay. Knowing she couldn't compete with Lonny in the pin-up category, she toned down the look she might have tried even as little as a week ago. The red suit had been far too flashy and besides, he'd seen the outfit both on and off.

She didn't need a reminder of the night he had rejected her. Almost brave enough now to be the real Vix, she dressed conservatively with a tiny dash of flash, wearing a little black dress with little black heels and a short pink jacket.

A little after seven, she stood on Jay's front porch and pressed his doorbell. Her heart began to pound the moment she heard his footsteps in the hallway. The door cricked and widened, and he stood there, his teeth flashed white in a smile as wide as the great outdoors. He looked all hunky male in his jeans, which he wore with a trendy yellow-striped cotton shirt. And he smelled deliciously clean.

"Hi." His khaki eyes searched hers. "Ready to go? Just a moment." He ducked inside his bedroom and came out wearing his leather jacket.

She stepped off the porch and he followed, shutting the door behind him. The day had been clear and hot but with the waning of the sun, the temperature had dropped. Summer had arrived with a whimper rather than a shout, but at this time of year, the weather always varied between too hot or slightly chilly.

With a resolute breath, she latched onto his arm and he walked her right past her car, pressing the control device he removed from his pocket. The door of the single garage attached to the house rolled up and he walked straight into a serious workshop, with a grease-stained concrete floor and a wall of shelves holding multicolored plastic boxes marked hinges, screws, wire, et cetera. In the center of the area sat a workbench piled high with woodcuts. Against this leaned a dark motorbike, flashy with chrome. He opened a compartment under the seat and waited for her to take the helmet he held out.

"You're not serious." She backed away from the hard protective hat.

"I sure am." He put on his.

"If this gives me helmet hair, you'll be sorry." She glanced at her straight skirt and sighed, taking the helmet. "I don't know if I'm brave enough."

"We're only travelling a block away and we wouldn't get a car park any closer than here. Would you rather walk?"

"I'd rather be brave enough to get onto the bike."

"Live dangerously." Laughing, he swung onto the machine and waited for her.

Nervously, she sat behind him and he started the engine, puttering out of the garage as the door closed behind them. He avoided her car and hit the street, the bike moving off with a roar of power.

She clutched him around the waist, her hands flat against his hard abdomen, resting her cheek against his warm, leather-clad shoulder, mainly for security. The bike had a sway she couldn't quite get used to and so she tried concentrating on the passing scenery, which stopped after crossing two narrow streets. He pulled up the bike in a tiny parking space near a seedy-looking hotel whose wide dark veranda shaded the asphalt footpath on the corner of Commercial Road. She stepped off the machine, her legs shaky, her skirt shorter than she would have liked, and pulled down the hem. Despairing of her carefully straightened hair, she removed the helmet, which he placed back into the compartment with his.

With his large hand on the center of her spine, he escorted her inside, across a dreadful patterned red carpet, probably chosen to hide stains. As well as failing this brief, the velvet pile had disappeared in a well-worn track to the bar in the first room off the dark main hall. The area smelled of hot chips and beer.

A pretty, twenty-something barmaid looked up and smiled. "Hi, JD," she said in an animated voice, pretending to wipe a glass while assessing the fit of his jeans. "What'll it be?"

"Two beers," he said without asking Vix. Then he turned to her. "Do you want the roast of the day or a mixed grill?"

"May I look at the menu?"

"That is the menu."

"Oh. A roast then, please."

"And two roasts." He handed over a fifty-dollar note to the barmaid.

"Take a table, and I'll bring everything over." The barmaid gave Jay two napkin-wrapped sets of knives and forks, and twenty dollars change.

As Vix eased herself into a vinyl-padded chair, she glanced at the billiard table in the corner and the towel along the bar. Except for the arguing drunken couple in the corner, most of the customers looked as if they'd stopped off for a drink after work, the men in tired suits, and the women in dresses or shirts and skirts. Although the pub looked as down-market as one could get, the atmosphere seemed upbeat. "Do you eat here often?" She dropped her bag to her feet.

"About once a week." He smiled at the barmaid, who placed two glasses of beer on the table.

Vix glanced at the froth on the beer and took her first sip, probably adding a white moustache to her helmet-hair. She swiped her tongue over her lip. "No doubt you get sick of cooking like the rest of us. I'm just discovering how tiring a working week can be, having now worked for two of them. How long have you been working?"

"I started at seventeen in the building trade. I've been doing set construction for three years. I wanted something I could do on weekends or nights, if need be. Set-building fit my brief. I can choose my hours."

"What do you have against regular hours?"

"Regular hours? That's what I do now and in another week or two, that's what I'll be doing for the rest of my life. Tomorrow is the last time I'll need a Thursday off."

She moistened her lips. Since he hadn't said why he needed a day off in the middle of the week, she didn't know if she should ask or wait to be told. "What do you do on Thursdays?" she asked tentatively.

His gaze dropped. "I'm learning all those tricks I need, like using a slide rule." He picked up his beer and downed half, and two very presentable roasts arrived. "The service is speedy when you arrive before the rush. Most people drink now and eat later."

"This looks delicious." She eyed roast pork with blistered crackling, accompanied by piled vegetables and apple. "You know the right places to eat, clearly."

Sipping at her beer, she began to eat, amazingly conscious of him. She noticed when his arm moved, when his head lifted, and when he smiled at her, the warm fuzzies took over. The meal finished quickly while he discussed the politics of the area and the beauty of the old Georgian buildings. She mentioned the irresponsibility of the local property owners who let their buildings collapse instead of renovating, a subject her father had touched on from time to time. Being a landowner himself, he couldn't understand the neglect. The conversation continued in a lovely getting-to-know you way until JD ordered coffee. After that, she could only think about racing him home and into bed, despite the early hour.

This time, prepared, she had brought fresh underwear and working clothes for tomorrow. The trip home on his roaring bike took minutes, and she wanted to rush him inside. She jittered from foot to foot while he settled his bike and locked the garage door. Her blood pounded loud enough to hear. She latched onto his arm, almost pulling him to the front door, where he stopped. Dead. Fumbled around for the key in his pocket and turned.

"I enjoyed our conversation tonight very much," he said in a formal voice. "I hope I see you again."

For a moment, she was taken aback...until she realized he was playing with the first date scenario. She smiled. "So, how about a kiss?"

He lowered his gaze demurely and shuffled his feet. "I don't usually kiss on the first date."

She slid her hand up his chest to the back of his neck, her thumb catching on his bristled jaw. He glanced at her with his tiger-eyes and she somehow wedged herself right up against his hard body. "You won't get a second date if you don't," she said, her voice husky. She lifted to her toes to have as much of him against her as possible.

His hands slid to her waist. "Okay, just one." He lowered his mouth to hers, his lips tickling across, again and again. His breath shortened, or hers did. His erection pressed into her belly.

Her flesh heated and her hand tightened around his neck. She dropped her handbag and lifted her other hand to join the first around his neck, lifting higher on her toes to rub herself against him. She wanted him so much that she couldn't breathe, couldn't think.

Without shifting his lips, he spun her around until she stood backed against his door. His hands grabbed her buttocks, lifting her off her feet, and he propped her upper body against the flaky wood. The door pressed into her shoulders. He nuzzled into her neck, ran his mouth to her jaw, and slowly teased his way back to her lips.

She tightened her ankles around his waist and she knew the expression on her face had gone soggy and stupid. She didn't want this, not to be emotionally involved. Day by day she not only wanted him more, but she liked him more. She knew then that he had planned this, every bit of it. He wanted her to like him more or he would just have taken what she offered: sex and only sex.

If he could tease her into doing what he wanted, he would be another Tim, though Tim hadn't teased. He'd simply given his orders. She couldn't let a man control her by foul means or fair, and so she took Jay's long slow kiss with desperation, knowing she had to finish him where she wanted to begin.

When his arm scooped under her bottom so that he could open the door, she ended the kiss. Steeling herself, she let her legs slide off his hips to the ground. He glanced at her.

"Wow," she said, her voice not quite as steady as she would have liked. "If that's your first date kiss, I can't wait for the second." She wriggled the hem of her skirt down, again, trying a limpid smile. "Sleep well."

Before she could let her second thoughts take hold, she backed and turned.

"Wouldn't you like a glass of milk?" He stood in the hallway, shoulders hunched, his hands plunged deep into his front pockets.

"Maybe after the second date." Drawing a deep breath and evading his stare, she fumbled in her bag for her car keys. "I'll see you on Friday at the shed."

He waited at the door until she backed her car out of his driveway.

* * * *

Jay stood among the final year students in his project group, dressed like the other guys in cotton slacks, a casual shirt, and a jacket. Unlike most, his jacket was his own, not borrowed. Unlike the other students, he worked for a living already.

He had given his talk for the group presentation, his final project before being awarded his Master of Architecture, which comprised his last two years of the five-year degree. This last part had taken him three years, one off while working in a full-time job to earn the money to qualify for a mortgage, and the other two working nights and weekends.

In the last two years, he had refined his technical ability, solved design problems, and developed various skills in sustainability and urban design, and more. During the next two years, he needed to gain work experience and to pass a final written exam before the Australian Institute of Architects recognized him as an accredited architect. His work experience, however, would come with a wage.

Three years ago, he would have done his work experience with Tremain's. Now, he had to find somewhere else. As long as his name hadn't been bandied about as a thug, he shouldn't have too much trouble in finding another architect willing to take him on. After the last speaker finished, he managed a wide grin and a fair bit of high-fiving before leaving the university grounds somewhat relieved. His job on the project had been the poster and, as the oldest, he had taken the role as the first speaker. He didn't want to let the others down, and he hadn't. Nor had they let him down. As a group, they were solid. He crossed North Terrace with the midday sun beating on his head and aimed for the side street, which housed Ilona's business.

He opened the glass door and walked through. The reception area had been painted a dark gray, matching the industrial carpet. A white couch and white table holding an arrangement of white flowers faced a doe-eyed receptionist, the front of whose desk displayed a laminated graphic of a sweaty rock band. He was waved through, past the closed white doors of a line of cubicles filled with low murmuring voices. Lonny sat in her dark gray office at the back.

She swiveled to face him, her shapely legs bare. "Pretty well on time," she said with her usual sultry smile. She stood, moved over to him, latched her long blue talons onto his arm, and kissed him on the cheek.

"This place is so impersonal. It's like a big classy factory."

"Everyone wants to look famous," Lonny said, her voice defensive. She scooped up her handbag.

"I won't knock success."

She frowned at him. "You shouldn't. I give you great haircuts. You look like a rock-star and that's why people stare at you."

"Is that so? Could you make me look like an architect? That's what I am as of today. Well, I will be when I get a job, and we both know that Tremain's is out."

"Not necessarily. Tim's been discredited by the divorce. He should have been discredited by having me on the side, but no one cared. I wasn't the first, and since his wife was so plain and ordinary, the common opinion was that he ought to have been allowed to have a bit of fun."

He ushered her out into the sunlight. "C'mon. She was used."

"She could have bought anyone she wanted." She tightened her lips.

"Presumably she had."

"Well, I don't have enough money to buy what I want," Lonny said, tossing her gleaming hair back over her shoulder.

"What do you want that you can't buy?"

"You," she said in a low voice. "It's always been you. I want you so much that I would take you on any terms."

He looked at her through narrowed eyes, still smarting about hearing lovely, funny Vix called plain and ordinary. "You don't want me. You only want to prove you can have anyone."

She stood frozen, staring at him, her face stark. Tears filled her eyes and her bottom lip trembled. "You should give us a chance. I'm your kind. She isn't. She'd be saying 'please' and 'thank you' and be putting flowers in vases all over the house. She would want to be seen in the most expensive restaurants and she would spend all your hard-earned money on designer clothes."

"Who?" he said roughly, though he had a good idea.

"Vix. What's that short for? Vixen? How private-school is that! Give me a break. In bed, she'd be anything but a vixen. I'm right, aren't I? Eight o'clock on a Sunday morning, and there she is, fresh and clean and cooking breakfast. Oh, so domestic!"

"You dropped by, did you?" he said grimly. "She didn't say a word."

"She wouldn't. She doesn't want you. All she wants is to walk on the wild side for a time. I bet you wouldn't take her home to meet your father." She flounced down the street, chin high.

He followed, with little to say. Even if his father were alive, he wouldn't introduce him to Vix and not out of shame, but rage. He caught up to Lonny. "I know she wants a walk on the wild side," he said, keeping his tone mild. He had seen her in this sort of mood before. Every now and again, she wanted to lash out, testing to see if he would forgive her. Since this was so routine, he no longer let her moods control him. "But for just a while I want flowers in vases all over my house. Why not?"

"God, Jay." She stopped, turning to him, tears spurting out of her eyes. "I would give you bloody flowers in vases. I would cook your bloody breakfast. I would have your babies."

He laughed. "Babies, even? And what would you name our second-born?"

"Something classy." She frowned. "Why the second born?"

He shrugged. Unlike Vix, she wouldn't have assumed he might want to abide by the new family tradition of using up the alphabet. Quockadile. Quockadile Dun Dee.

With a silly smile on his face, he escorted Ilona to the expensive restaurant she insisted on being seen in wearing her designer clothes. Not once in all the time he had known her had she gotten her clothes smeared with paint and not once had she helped him move furniture. If she knew how to upholster, she wouldn't offer to do that for him either. She had the princess-complex she thought Vix had.

Fortunately, though, she didn't realize Vix was short for Victoria and she didn't recognize Tim's ex-wife. He wouldn't have liked that because he didn't want Vix to know that he had. Or she might suspect his motive for wanting to be her man for a while.

* * * *

Vix hoped Jay didn't think she walked out on him the night before. Asking for a kiss would have shown she didn't, but she still worried that she might have acted a little too much out of character.

With him away and Steve in charge, her working day was as usual but without the added sexual tug of Jay's presence. She painted the changing-huts with alternate aqua and yellow doors as in the Melbourne production while she plotted the family portraits she needed to begin for the *Who Wants to be a Millionaire* scene. The designer had told her he wanted portraits of the heroine's parents and a few assorted ancestors. She had photos of the actors who played the parents, but she could use her imagination for the other relatives. A few regional-prominent identities should be subtly aged, she decided. Meanwhile, Trent searched out suitable frames.

In the afternoon, she stiffened more fabric for the leaves in the outdoor scenes. Because making the leaves was so labor intensive, she did parts of the job whenever she needed a break from painting, or from thinking. The greenery would be glued onto sheer fabric in strips, so that the leaves would move when the actors brushed past. The warehouse wallowed in a momentary silence broken only by the buzz of a mobile phone and a low voiced conversation. Finally, she heard a loud shout of, "Whoopee!"

"What happened?" she heard Trent call.

"I've got another date," Steve yelled. Then he did a slow, shoulder-swinging walk to Jay's makeshift desk where Vix sat. "Did you hear that?" he asked looking down at her with a blue-steel expression, a casual hand resting on his hip.

"They heard you in the outer suburbs. I gather getting another date is something unusual for you." She gave him a wide grin.

"Nah. But getting another date with Lonny is. I had a couple more than a month ago, and I thought I was in with a chance but…you know." He lifted his shoulders helplessly. "She kinda brushed me off. Then we met up again last week and now today she's called me. I can take her out again if I wear a long-sleeved shirt. She doesn't like the tats. This one"—he pointed to the face on his bare upper arm—"is her."

"Is it a good likeness?" Vix peered closely at dark blue face that could have been anyone at all. "Well, sort of."

"The tattooist copied her photo," Steve said, craning to look at his upper arm. "It seemed like a good idea at the time."

"I suspect most tattoos do. He's got the shape of her face right."

His thick black eyebrows drew together. "Do you know Lonny?"

And suddenly, Vix realized she'd been indiscreet. She'd promised not to let Jay know she'd met Lonny and now she'd blurted the news to Steve. "Not really. I only saw her once."

"Where? How did you know it was her?"

"She introduced herself last Sunday morning at Jay's house. I was, um, helping him paint his main room."

"Sunday morning." Steve breathed out, his satisfied expression dying a slow death. His eyes clouded over. "I guess she slept over, hey?" he said, rearranging the pencil on the desk.

"No." Hot with embarrassment, Vix cooled her face with her arm. "I got there first. She dropped in."

"Oh." Steve kept staring at her until she thought he suspected she had spent the night. "You sure?"

"I'm sure. They're only friends."

"That's what they say." He sighed. "No reason to lie, is there?"

"I wouldn't have thought he was a lying sort of man."

"He's not." He trailed away, his beefy shoulders drooping.

She could have kicked herself, but she understood. He and she were of a kind. Neither wanted to see Jay and Lonny together and probably each for the same reason.

* * * *

On Friday, Vix tried to treat Jay casually, but the truth was that she couldn't have been more conscious of anyone. The mere glimpse of him thrilled her, sent her heart vibrating like a wrongly positioned screwdriver bit. When he came near, her blood raced and her breathing ached through her chest.

"Do I have to make dates with you or can I assume I'm the only man in your life right now?" he asked into the back of her neck as she leaned over her first sketch of the heroine's grandmother. His breath tickled. "That looks like an elderly Nichole Kidman."

"Good. I wanted someone elegant. Do you think it would be too much to use Keith Urban as the grandfather?" She shivered a smile as his lips explored just under her ear.

"Answer my question first."

"It's insulting. I'm sleeping with you, sort of. I'd hardly be dating someone else."

"It's the sort of that's confusing me. You're sort of not sleeping with me. How about tonight?"

She hauled in a breath and turned her face around to look at him. "To sleep with you, or not to sleep with you?"

"That is the question. It's Friday. We don't have to do much sleeping. I'd like to do the other thing a few times." His fingers lightly brushed her cheek, and he gave the slow sort of smile that would make any red-blooded woman seethe with lust.

"How about my place? Yours gets a bit crowded at times." She thought she should hint about Lonny before Steve said something.

His lips pressed together in a firm line. "So I heard yesterday. I didn't know Lonny had dropped by but when she told me, I took my key back."

"So, you see Lonny on Thursdays."

"Not usually. And...no, not Keith Urban. That makes it personal. Another actor would be better. That makes it theatrical."

She pondered his logic and nodded. "Should I cook dinner?"

"Is that routine for a second date?"

"Yes," she said firmly. "You cooked before the first date and so I'm sure I can cook on the second."

He nodded and left, which meant she had to mentally review what she had in the fridge and what she could pick up on the way home. She picked up two steaks because he was a guy and guys ate steak. Her fridge held various ingredients for salad and her father kept her wine supply current.

She activated her front gates just before seven and a few minutes later she heard his motorbike puttering into the drive. Although she wanted to run to the door, she didn't want to seem as if she was waiting for him, and so she let him ring the doorbell while she moved the flowers off the dining room table. Such formality might put him off, which was a pity. She liked flowers everywhere.

"Nice garden," he said as she opened the door. "Did you do the design?"

"Just the shapes and colors. I don't know too much about plants."

"I'm pleased to hear you can't do everything." He began to walk into her. "Have you started cooking yet?"

"No. Only the prep." She backed, her hands on his shoulders and her querying gaze examining the expression on his face, which was inscrutable.

"Good." With a grin, he reached out and snatched her into his arms. While he undid the long zipper on her dress, he kept his lips on hers, and he backed her farther into the living room.

Her dress dropped onto carpet close to the couch and her bra followed. Then his shirt, which he jerked over his head. Before he tossed her onto the couch, he had removed her undies and she wasn't sure if he had completely removed his trousers before he entered her.

And, actually, she didn't care.

Chapter 11

Jay opened his eyes. The sunlight filtered through the vine-leaf covered pergola outside the two French doors Vix had in her bedroom instead of a window. A gently wavering dapple reflected on the walls. He stretched, utterly content, noting that Vix slept with one hand under her cheek, an endearing position that suited her. For a while, he stared at her, noting her delicate eyelashes and the lock of pale hair that twisted across her beautiful mouth.

He contemplated tickling her face with her hair, but decided he didn't want to wake her, not yet. Even now, he couldn't believe he lay naked in her bed, in her large white beautiful bedroom, and he needed to get his bearings. Comparing this room to his was like comparing a palace to a dugout.

Her floorboards were polished, as his would be in a few weeks, but there any resemblance ended. A large red-and-black Persian rug, possibly an antique, carpeted her floor. She had mixed mainly dark wood antique furniture with white painted side-tables holding bronze art deco lamps. Only two paintings hung on her walls, each a light-filled outback scene framed in red. Nothing could have been simpler or more elegant. Maybe taste and style was inbred. He hoped not because one day he should be able to mix and match the way she did.

He sat up, rubbing his hair, contemplating dressing and leaving. Her white quilted bedspread had been hurriedly thrown off her white-sheeted bed last night and his jocks might lurk underneath. In a trail from the bed to the door, he spotted his jeans and his shirt. His shoes would be in the dining room or the hallway. Untidy, yes, but a formerly unknown urgency had possessed him last night. Perhaps his fear of losing her multiplied these thoughts. The moment she found out who he was, she would dump him. A woman like her would remain loyal to her family, no matter what.

His thoughts stark, he slid carefully out of her bed, collected his shirt, underwear, and jeans and strode into her on-suite bathroom. One day he would have a bathroom like hers, but not in his current house, which was too small. In the meantime, he enjoyed her shower and her thick white fluffy towels. He didn't shave.

She was still sleeping when he went back into the bedroom. He sat on the side of the bed, hoping she might wake up, not knowing whether to stay or discreetly leave. He didn't know if she would want him to stay, not now that she'd experienced the full deal before dinner and three times during the night. He was under no illusion that she wanted him for anything other than sex. Had she been anyone else, he might not have minded, but she was Vix—one of a kind, talented, generous, and much more sexy than she thought. She'd chosen the wrong husband was all.

And then she stirred and her eyes opened. She gave the dazzling smile that turned up at either end. "Hi."

"Hi."

"You look fresh and clean. Delicious." She gave a contented smile, sat up, and glanced at the glass doors. "It's late. Normally I would go to the gym for a hearty workout. Would you say last night counts?"

"As exercise?" He pretended to consider. "I don't know about you, but I'm pretty sure I maintained a racing heartbeat for quite a while."

She dropped her gaze and toyed with the sheet covering. "And now you need a sustaining breakfast. I can't make you wait until I've showered. Help yourself to anything you like in the kitchen. I have cereal, fruit, yogurt, eggs if you like, no bacon, and plenty of bread."

He stood. "Okay…but if you want help in the shower, call me."

She made a mischievous purse of her lips. "The newspaper will be on the front lawn if you want something to read while you eat."

Having been blessed by a far from awkward morning-after, he left to raid her kitchen, deciding not to be impressed by her expensive house and valuable possessions. If Tim had paid for them and lost everything in the divorce, well done her. If she owned them herself, envy wouldn't make a better man of Jay.

He ate, after spotting a loose shelf in her bathroom-sized pantry that he could fix and a crooked curtain rail in her sitting room. When she arrived, smelling good and looking even better in burgundy jeans and a soft citrus top, he said, "Do you have a set of tools anywhere?"

"What do you plan to make?" She poured muesli into a flower-patterned bowl and reached for the carton of milk he had left out.

"Fix. Everything that needs fixing. What else other than the curtain rail and the shelf in the pantry?"

"There's a wobbly tile in the spare bathroom." She brought her breakfast over to the table where he sat with the newspaper spread out like a respectable married man. "I bought the glue and the grout but I didn't get around to it. So, do we tell the guys we're dating?"

"Maybe not." He rubbed his chin. "As a matter of fact, I think being a twosome in a work environment is a bit awkward."

"That's what I was thinking. The guys would start being careful about what they said around us. Anyway, it's nice to share a secret with you. What do you plan on doing today?"

"Whatever you like." He grinned, knowing by now that she liked what he liked.

He had a meandering sort of day, doing odd jobs, making love, eating, making love, laughing, and finally taking a hand-in-hand walk around the botanical gardens, which he assumed was her way of motivating him into fixing his own garden. They spent that night at his house, so that he could change his clothes, and the next because he realized she could keep her car in the garage if he moved a few things around, and therefore not be seen when he was picked up in the morning by Steve.

* * * *

"How was your weekend, Vix?" Steve stood in front of Vix, smiling like a man who'd had a bacon and eggs breakfast. He had shaved off his goatee. Added to that, he wore a working shirt with the sleeves rolled down to his elbows.

"Fantastic. I'm thinking yours was, too. The clean-shaven look suits you."

"You think so?" He rubbed seeking fingers over his chin. "I feel kind of naked."

"You look kind of handsome."

"Seems the key to success is hiding my tattoos." He glanced at his colorful lower arms, his lips wryly pressed together.

"You don't need to be humble about your arm decorations. You were expressing your inner artist."

Steve looked horrified. Jay would have laughed. And at that moment, she knew she had moved on from Tim. Completely. Her first thought had been to compare Steve to Jay instead of relating everything in her life to her ex-husband. Mentally, as well as physically, she had left the man who had in so many ways betrayed her. How amazing that a few bouts of incredible sex could change a woman's whole way of thinking.

"Inner artist?" He considered. "Maybe I can use that. Yeah."

"So, your big date was a success?"

He nodded, his grin wide. "Pretty good. I don't want to brag, though JD's spitting chips. I reckon he thought he didn't have any competition."

"Spitting chips, how?" Vix put her paintbrush down, momentarily nervous. She'd kissed Jay good-bye no longer than two hours ago when he left for work with Steve, and he'd been very pleased with himself then. A betting person would put money on him not giving a thought to Lonny.

"You don't know his style, but he likes to pretend he doesn't care. Today he's looking pretty serious, wouldn't you say?"

"I think he looks about the same as usual."

"He only looks serious when he's worried."

"Maybe it's work related. Speaking of which, will you have time today to cut out the bay for me?" Vix planned to paint trees and bushes as a panoramic frame around the cyclorama, called the cyc, the last screen before the black wall of the stage. On this, the lighting engineer could project moving ripples of water, representing the bay that would form the background for all the outdoor scenes in the show.

"I reckon Jay will get Kell onto it. He'll be here soon if his dates this weekend didn't take too much out of him. He finished his last job before Christmas. After that, he and Luke will be taking a two-week break. Tradies! They've got it good. We'll be working except on Christmas day."

"Everyone?"

"We need to have the set finished by January the twenty-fifth." He left to find the sheets of composite wood on which Vix had sketched various trees and bushes, while she sat happily painting a marble finish on the fireplace for *High Society*'s sitting room scene.

Kell arrived looking as inscrutable as usual and with barely a consenting nod, he began cutting out the bay. Like Jay, he had the ability to do any job required. Unlike Jay, he applied himself with an intense concentration. He seemed to lose himself in work. Each of the Dee brothers had an amazing work ethic, almost matched by Steve and Trent. As a team, they couldn't be bettered. She counted herself lucky to be with this team for her first job.

She had already painted the heroine's parents and her grandmother, and she thought she would use Geoffrey Rush for the grandfather. Given more time, she would paint Steve and Trent in regency outfits as haughty forebears, which she mentioned during the tea break.

"Do I get a beard?" Trent asked, his elbows on the bare table and his coffee mug slanting dangerously in his fingers.

"You get sideburns," Vix said to the man who didn't even have side hair.

"That'd be right," he said glumly, but she knew he was pleased to have been acknowledged her way. She enjoyed being with these men who, with the exception of Jay, indulged what they saw as her every nerdy whim. Nothing would have surprised her less than to be patted on the head. Had they known who her father was, she would have been treated as James's daughter, with a small amount of contempt mixed with a large amount of envy. With these men, she had to prove herself, and because they respected her work, she thought she might have.

"What about me?" Steve looked nervous. "I don't want one of those white wigs with curls."

"Darn. Are you sure?"

He sighed. "Do what you have to."

Jay gave her a chin-down, eyes-up glance of tolerance, and her heart lurched. Had anyone ever looked at her that way, as if she was just Vix and completely acceptable?

"Do you want me to paint you, too?" Her voice trembled slightly.

His eyes glinted and creased at the outside corners but he didn't answer. "Back to work, guys."

The men shuffled off but Jay stopped Vix from leaving, too, by taking hold of her left wrist as she went to move past him. She glanced into his eyes and he took her breath away. She slid into his arms.

"Kiss me, you adorable idiot," he said in a low voice.

She didn't protest about the insult. She kissed him, and he kissed her, taking his time. "Can't wait for tonight. My place. I'll let you paint me with soap."

She spent the longest working day of her life shaky with anticipation, leaving early and packing a small bag with fresh clothes for the morning.

Not long after Jay would have arrived home, she drove into his garage and walked in the back door the way Lonny used to.

"Do you want to eat first?" Jay took her bag and tossed it onto his couch.

In answer, she stepped out of her shoes and unbuttoned her working shirt. While she stripped to nothing, he did, too. He smiled, gloriously naked, and guided her into the bathroom. "This could be a long shower."

He washed her shoulders, her back, and her buttocks, taking his time. Then, he turned her around and soaped her breasts and nipples and, taking even longer after she turned back, between her legs, apparently not noticing her clear need as she circled her arms around his neck, offering him a desperate kiss. He accepted this without undue loss of control, though his body had certainly taken note.

Although she didn't know if she could play his games and win, she leaned back and, shaking, she tipped a handful of shower gel into her palms. Keeping her expression bland, she slicked the liquid over his neck and shoulders, massaging down his arms until she twined her fingers with his, easing between, and letting her palms slide against his. He seemed relaxed but his breathing sped up. And then he cheated. He lifted the backs of her hands to the tiled wall, held them there, and pressed his hard body against hers.

"I'm not as good at this as you are," he said, his mouth inches from hers. "Any touch, and I'll give in."

"You didn't before when I wanted you to. Take your punishment like a man."

Breathing out, he eased off. "I am. Men aren't sporting about being teased."

His expression changing to one of pure determination, he kissed her until she hooked one of her legs onto his hip, silently begging for more. With a palm against the tiles to keep his balance, he slowly entered her while she clutched onto him, laughing while the water sprayed all over her face.

Naturally, by the time she emerged from the shower, happily sated, her hair dripped in tails over her shoulders. "I wish you had a hair dryer." She rubbed at her hair, watching while he combed his back from his face. His strong features fascinated her.

"I suppose you wish I had a lot of things."

She glanced lower. "Somehow I seem to be able to settle for what you have."

His mouth moved into a satisfied smirk, which so appealed to her that she grabbed him and kissed him. The kisses lasted a long, long time. Kissing Jay was a totally erotic experience. He liked to tease and he liked her to tease back. He kissed like a man who loved women and who had all the time in the world to experience whatever titillation she offered.

Later, after they'd eaten and had a rudimentary conversation about the upholstery for his art deco chairs, and inspected the finish on the floorboards in the garage he had cut and polished for the cupboard doors, she realized she shared every facet of his life. She worked with him, she played with him, she slept with him, and she agreed with him about food, drink, colors, and designs. Sex couldn't have been more wonderful than with Jay. The relationship she had with him was the one she should have had with her husband but she'd been too young or too immature to choose a grown-up man.

But Jay would never be her husband. He would never fit into her world and she would never fit into his. She'd been there, done that, and had failed to fit. Now she was older and wiser.

She fell asleep with her face in his shoulder and her leg over his.

* * * *

Although Vix stayed over most nights, she hadn't moved in with Jay. Other than with Ilona, he'd never lived with a woman. Living with Lonny had been like living with his little brothers. He'd cooked for her, cleaned up after her, and waited up for her. She'd been a mess when she had broken up with Tim. Regardless of what she said, she had expected to marry Tim. She hadn't revealed all to Jay, but he deduced from her various comments that having once married for money, Tim meant to continue on that course and keep Lonny on the side. Jay was pleased that Lonny wouldn't accept that.

He sanded his art deco chairs, which he had stripped and planned to finish with a layer or two of French polishing since he had seen satinwood underneath the paint as Vix had guessed. Tonight, Vix was attending a class reunion, which would do her good. In the past weeks, she'd only socialized with the team and him, and although at this stage of their relationship he could happily keep her to himself, he knew he also had to just as happily share. He wouldn't be seeing her until tomorrow and he wanted the chairs finished by then so that she could work on the upholstery.

He laughed to himself. She had everything money could buy and yet she'd spent practically the whole month saving him money by doing jobs for him. He'd never been in love before, and Vix was a very special girl. When the time came, he hoped he would be able to let her go without trying to take her back again.

* * * *

Vix took a two-hour lunch break and had her hair trimmed to shoulder length. Sitting in front of the hairdresser's mirror, she stared at herself, swishing her head, liking the fact that her hair swayed without being caught on her shoulders. Now, no one could say she looked like Lonny.

Lately, she had found constantly straightening her hair a time waster when she had so many things to do that were more interesting than worrying about her appearance. So now, finally, she looked like herself rather than the sort of woman who would interest the sort of man who didn't interest her. Since the summer heat curled her hair, the hairdresser had facilitated that. Vix thought she looked younger and brighter when she arrived back at the warehouse, but naturally not one of the guys noticed.

"How was the reunion with the girls?" Jay asked, leaving the others and strolling over when he spotted her.

"Guilt-making, initially. After I was married, I stopped seeing my old friends. Unbelievable as it sounds, my husband asked that of me, and I did as he asked. My two besties from school were there last night and they forgave me instantly. One is married with a baby and the other is still single, like me."

"So, you see yourself as single?" He lifted his eyebrows.

"If I'm not married, I'm single." She planted her hands on his hips, challenging him with a smile.

"So, I am, too." He sounded miffed. "Single with benefits. Will I see you tonight? I finished the chairs."

"Great. That will give me something interesting to do at your place." Staring straight into his eyes, she laughed with the confidence of a woman who could now use sex as recreation.

He sighed and she enjoyed his air of amused tolerance. When he left, she stared after him, momentarily guilty. She could tease him about sex now, but she appreciated the other aspects of their relationship just as much and she knew he did, too. He liked that she could make and do, and she appreciated that he could. She liked that he didn't care about money, but he didn't need to. He was self-sufficient. She loved watching him work as much as she loved working herself.

After a meal of grilled salmon and salad with him that night, she sat on the floor in front of his art deco chairs, inspecting the material they had chosen together, a suede striped in two shades of brown. Jay had stripped the seats of the dusty old material and removed the webbing from the undersides. She tacked on the new webbing while he tried not to help her. She could see his hands twitch with the effort.

"You can finish this while I get the curved needle ready to sew the springs to the webbing."

He gave her one of his ah-ha glances and took over, hammering quickly and efficiently. "What are you doing for Christmas?"

"Steve said you guys will only be taking off Christmas day. I have to go to the country for Christmas. My father always spends summer in the Barossa and I haven't seen the rest of the family since I started this job. He expects me to stay for at least three to four days. I plan to leave town on the twenty-fourth, and be back at the warehouse on the twenty-eighth. What are you doing?" She began to sew the springs to the webbing.

"Sherry does Christmas day for us. Do you want a coffee?"

"Water, thanks."

He disappeared into the garage when she began on the seats, first arranging the padding, then stapling the lining, and finally she tacked the suede upholstery fabric on top. That done, she neatened the underneath, using calico to conceal the webbing. She glued on the braid, and then she upholstered the center of the chair backs, since the strips needed nothing other than that and the brown braid edging. When she had finished, she went outside to see what he was doing.

He had made new cupboard doors for the kitchen out of reclaimed wood—so far, only four. At the rate he worked, he would have the lot finished before Christmas. She hugged him and one thing led to another. Before she had time to appreciate his urgent foreplay, he whisked her back inside for one of his glorious bad-boy sessions.

She had planned to go home that night, but for one reason or another, she stayed the whole weekend again. On Monday morning, Jay was picked up by Steve, as usual. Keeping the relationship quiet had begun to be a chore. Life would be easier for her if the guys knew about her relationship with Jay, but she would lose the friendships she had begun to cherish. From being one of the guys, she would be reclassified as the boss's woman. Most of her life had been spent as the boss's daughter. She no longer wanted to concede to ownership.

With half an hour to wait until she could leave, too, she pottered around his house. The sitting room was finished but for the window coverings and possibly a few pictures on the walls. Though she said so herself, the room looked design perfect. She knew he planned to do his bedroom next and she agreed that the other two could wait. However, somehow she'd never wandered into either room and so she did.

The one he called the second bedroom held a large single bed, a '50s-style dressing table and a matching wardrobe, both irredeemable. The bed was made-up with a yellow patterned spread but no longer covered by the books he had mentioned previously. The third bedroom held the books, piled insecurely on the floor, and a large desk containing a computer, a printer, and folder of printouts. Rolls of paper occupied one corner with sheets of cardboard and detailed drawings of various buildings, apparently diagrams of old sets. One day she would love to see what he had built, but today she had room renovating in mind. If he wanted a nice study, he didn't need to do much to this room other than polish the floor, paint the walls, and add solid shelving.

Thinking, she remembered her father had a couple of sets of red-gum shelves in his Barossa shed that had once graced the offices of Tremain's. He had deemed these too good to toss out willy-nilly and would be pleased to donate them to a worthy cause, or so she imagined. She would ask him when she went to the country house on Thursday. Also, she needed to decide on a Christmas present for Jay, nothing extravagant. Although she would have loved to buy him a new wardrobe of clothes, that would be like buying him, and she wouldn't buy a man again. If she couldn't earn him herself, he wasn't worth having.

The thought stopped her in her tracks. She wanted to keep him. She hadn't fallen in love in a couple of months. Not at all. She'd fallen in love in a single day. She had watched him work and play, and she had been totally charmed. Only now did she realize she had loved him from the start and she couldn't deny this to herself any longer.

She'd never had more in common with anyone in her life. He was the perfect man for her in every way but one. Background. That shouldn't be insurmountable. Her father could set him up in his own business. Jay was canny enough to make a success of himself with backing. But would her father agree? Would Jay? He was certainly a proud man and likely wouldn't accept being bought. And since she had bought her first husband, she had real qualms about having to buy her second.

Of course, neither of them had mentioned love. She certainly hadn't. Nor would she until and unless she decided that apart from companionability she provided and the regular sex, he wanted a forever relationship. The only important question was did Jay actually love her, too?

Chapter 12

Melissa Tremain, Vix's stepmother, opened the door. "Darling," she drawled, her welcoming smile showing her square white teeth. For a woman of her age, mid-forties, she looked marvelous. She could have passed for mid-thirties had she dressed younger but she wore designer clothes, tonight wearing a free-flowing black skirt and a tailored cream silk blouse, both probably with French labels. The long hallway of the country mansion loomed behind her, highlighting her stylish, blond jaw-length hair. "You look gorgeous. Doesn't she look gorgeous, James?"

Vix's gray-blond father, standing behind with his hand on his wife's shoulder said, "Yes, dear." Wearing light trousers and a shirt in the same blue color as his eyes, he winked at Vix.

Pushing between them, Sebastian, her young half-brother yelled, "Vix. Granny is cooking. Come to the kitchen with me." He snatched at her hand.

"Your father will bring in your bags," Melissa said, stepping neatly aside.

"Kiss first." Vix kissed her father and Melissa and her small, blond, determined brother before she was hauled down the wide passage to the kitchen right at the end of the house. The first South Australian Tremain had settled here in 1856, having made his fortune in the fertile Barossa Valley.

Now the diminished holding grew grapes for Vix's father's hobby boutique winery. James also ran a few token cows and horses and he kept hens as well as an extensive vegetable garden. Melissa grew roses for the inside of the house where the original old rooms were large and gracious and the new additions were larger and more gracious, the two parts connected by a glass atrium through which Vix passed to the enormous marble-floored kitchen.

Her grandmother was in her middle seventies, a good-looking, trim woman, and as she said herself, "well preserved." Margaret Tremain put on her discreet makeup at first light in the morning and she never had one smooth gray hair out of place. She never had a chip in her bright nail polish, and she dressed like a woman with an extensive income. Her high-necked citrus lace blouse coordinated perfectly with her slim-fitting gray skirt. Vix had been led to believe her own mother had been equally fashion conscious.

Vix didn't wear nail polish now. Paint messed with manicured hands. "Granny. Merry Christmas." She hugged and kissed the older woman.

Margaret leaned back. "Well. Not only do you look beautiful, but you look happy. Working must agree with you."

"I wasn't any more idle while I was married than you are," Vix said in a voice of mock outrage. "What are you making?"

"Gingerbread," Sebastian shrieked from the sidelines. "They all forgot."

"But you don't like gingerbread." Vix glanced at him with a smile.

"I'll be in grade two next year," he said with a repressive frown. "I'm a bit more grown up than I was last Christmas."

"I've noticed. Smart jeans! I bet you wouldn't have worn them when you were five."

"Well," he said looking down at his jeans. "I got them when I was five but I was almost six. Can I squash the dough for you, Granny?"

Margaret placed the stool, Sebastian kneeled on the seat, and with great concentration he made a lumpy mass worthy of a six-year-old. He lost interest when offered the rolling pin and left for other older-boy pursuits, like taking off his new red sneakers and skidding in his socks down the polished hall. Meanwhile, Vix and her lovely granny made gingerbread men and caught up on the latest doings of each other.

Melissa liked dinner to be formal, and so Vix changed out of her travelling clothes into a sleeveless floral top and an olive green flowing skirt. She spent a happy Christmas Eve with her family, certain Jay would fit in here. An uncomplicated man, he could talk about world affairs, politics, and various incidentals without unnecessary words or wandering into personalities. He didn't have the gossip gene she so disliked and he had a rare ability to draw people into conversations.

She would never be ashamed of him in company, even with his shaggy-cut hair, his work boots, and his pilled shirts. He wasn't a pushy type. He eased in and he relaxed people. She thought her father would probably like him, being the same.

Not until the day after Christmas did she have time to talk to her father alone. She asked him if she could have the shelves in the shed for a friend.

"Of course. When do you want them delivered?"

"I'll need to make sure he wants them first, not that I think he won't. He trusts my taste."

"He?"

"The set construction manager. I'm helping him redecorate his house."

"He couldn't find anyone better. You've always had a good eye for color. What does his wife think about him taking advice from a smart, beautiful blonde?" He pushed his hands into his pockets and raised his eyebrows at her.

She laughed. "That's your subtle way of asking if he's single. Yes, he is. All the guys I work with are single except the youngest, who also has three children, and he's younger than me."

"So, tell me about your work."

"I'm the only woman working on the set and so naturally I'm treated like a princess. I barely need to lift a finger. They fetch and carry and do everything I want, five of them. I've been very spoiled. They all have special skills. For instance, the youngest, Luke, is a plumber and he has constructed intricate piping for the swimming pool on the set. The pool will look real but it's just a visual trick. His brother, Kell, has made or modified most of the furniture we need. And Trent. He's amazing. He has been cutting out various leaves and trees for me with a jigsaw and so intricately that they're almost works of art. Each of the guys has a different skill. They like what they do, and that's infectious."

He nodded. "I can't think of the last time I saw you with that glow of happiness."

"Why wouldn't I be happy when I am treated like a goddess? I was used to being with people who made me feel gauche and childish. Now, I think I'm a grown woman with interesting ideas. If I'm insecure about any of my colors or finishes, I get bolstered up with large amounts of admiration. We're all about same age at the warehouse, which is I suppose why we get along so well."

"I'm sure they appreciate you as much as we do." He gave her a doting-father smile. "Your enthusiasm makes you very endearing. You'd lost that for a time."

She moistened her throat. "I'm enjoying helping with Jay's house, too. Oh, and I mixed a color for Luke's house and his wife loves it."

"I can't wait to see the show, but I'll only be looking at the sets, of course."

"Of course." She laughed. "I haven't been to a rehearsal yet and so I don't know how good the cast is. All I can recommend is the set."

"Your grandmother, with Melissa and I, will be coming to the first night. I have room for plenty more guests in the box, if you want to join us or invite anyone."

She hesitated. "I've talked the others into seeing the show after we have bumped-in, and so we'll be at the last dress rehearsal. Steve knows he will hate it. He says it freaks him out when a guy is talking on the stage and suddenly bursts into song. He said in real life a guy wouldn't be able to make up a tune and all the words on the spot, no matter how much in love he is."

He chuckled. "I think you have to be brought up with musical theater to appreciate the finer points. You were, and you do. You don't have to let me know about the box but we would love to enjoy your success with you."

"The guys don't know I'm your daughter," she said, awkwardly pulling at her fingers. "Maybe none have ever heard of you, but the press has and if I'm seen with you, I'll get a mention about painting the set and…I don't want to be your daughter who painted the set. If I'm mentioned, I want it to be because I did something special."

He caught her gaze, nodded slowly, and turned to the wall of the shed. "So, do these shelves look like the kind of thing you want for your set construction manager?"

She hugged him. "I'm pretty sure they're the kind of thing he would appreciate. He knows quality when he sees it, and he doesn't waste a thing. He made his kitchen cupboard doors from old floorboards and his sound system hides in an old cedar wardrobe. You would have to pay a thousand dollars for something like that in a vintage revival shop. The house is going to look fabulous when it's finished, but he probably won't get much for it when he sells."

"Why not? Renovated houses are usually good sellers."

She lifted her shoulders. "The house is in Port Adelaide. Prices there are so low it's ridiculous. From the end of his street, you can see the masts of the tall ships tethered along the dock. Wherever you look are old heritage buildings, most falling apart. The main streets are beautifully paved, though, and some renewal seems to be happening. We took a walk along the dock one evening, and the water is so clear there you can see the bottom. Sometimes, the dolphins come to the edge to say hello. It ought to be a great tourist area, but it's usually quiet."

"Jay," he said, a crease between his eyebrows. "Is he a Port Adelaide local?"

"Born and bred at the port." She smiled. "He looks rather dangerous at first glance because he has a scar on his face from here to here." She ran her finger from the edge of her mouth to under her eye. "But he's the gentlest person imaginable. All the guys are. They went to school together. If they're not careful, they'll give the place a good reputation."

Her father smiled. "Will you be working with the same team if you take other set jobs?"

"Jay has been doing some course or other related to building. He said he is going to work full-time next year and so I won't be working with him again, but I might be working with the others, that is, if I am reemployed."

And if she had done a good enough job, she might be offered a job as a set designer. Then, she would be self-supporting for the first time in her life. The idea swelled her head with pride. For the first time, she would actually be herself and worthy of a gorgeous guy like Jay.

* * * *

Jay's shoulders tensed as nine AM arrived. He examined one thing and then another, as nervous as a builder standing on a three-legged trestle. He didn't know if Vix might have mentioned his name to her father. If so, she would have found out about him and might not return on the day she said she would return, though he had the idea that even if she never wanted to speak to him again she would finish the job she had started. He couldn't see her leaving anyone in the lurch. Not Vix. Not the most responsible, reliable, and loveable woman in the world.

The warehouse door had been left open and he heard her car arrive. Meaning to look busy and not be waiting for her, he strode to the workbench area where Trent was cutting the outline of the bay Vix had designed, leaf by leaf, with the jigsaw. His work was intricate and beautifully finished.

"It's a shame there's not a lot of need for this sort of thing," Jay said, yet again impressed by Trent's new work ethic. Trent used to be a bricklayer not known for finishing a whole row before he wanted a break.

Trent paused and looked at him. "I'm thinking I could make some interesting trellises. Arty. I might be able to find a market if I mocked up a few at home."

"I never thought I would hear you use the word arty. And you are a wood artist, no doubt about it. Show this stuff to Kell. He might let you use his lathe if you ever want to do a bit of wood turning."

Trent gave him a pleased smile and at that moment the car door outside slammed. Steve and Tent put down their tools. Vix had only been away for three working days and already the guys thought her arriving back was an event, which gave Jay the opportunity to stroll to the door to greet her when her shadow entered before her. "Good Christmas?" he asked, his mouth dry with apprehension.

"The best. Hi, everyone." Vix gave him a special smile before she glanced at the others and he breathed out, knowing she hadn't heard a word about him. "I hope you people haven't finished the whole thing without me."

"Nearly," Steve said, trying to sound grumpy, but his face was creased with a grin. "Slacker. You'll have to paint fast to catch up to us."

"I brought bribes. Do I need bribes? Should I say presents or bribes?"

"Bribes." Jay laughed. He wanted to grab her, swing her around, and kiss her until she begged for mercy.

"In the back of the car. Could you carry them in for me? I've got a few in my bag, but I couldn't carry the bottles."

The word bottles had the guys ready to carry, and between them they brought in five boxes marked Maintree Wines. "Share them with Kellen and Luke. I didn't know who would like what and so I got a selection."

Jay appreciated the looks on the faces of the others as they read the labels, The Village Smithy, Under the Spreading Chestnut, Blowing Bellows, et cetera. He had seen the label before when Lonny had brought a bottle to his house. He hadn't connected Tremain with Maintree was all.

"You shouldn't have spent all that money," Steve said, his tone amazed. "Not on us."

"I didn't," she said with a naughty smile. "They're freebies. I got lots of food, too: pates, nuts, cheeses, pickled fruit, dried fruit, cakes. And loads of fresh fruit: mandarins, lemons, cherries, apricots, plums."

"How come?" Clearly Trent didn't believe that anyone could have hundreds of dollars worth of freebies.

"I spent half my life in the Barossa and so I know the makers and growers of most of these things. It's good publicity to offer free samples. I bet you've never had this pate before, for instance."

"These yobos have never had any pate before." Jay leaned back, crossed his arms, and laughed.

"Well, I'll do a couple of hours of painting and then I'll prepare us a party."

"Speaking of parties..." Steve stood in front of her, his expression hopeful. "You were away when we decided. Sherry is giving a party on New Year's Eve. She wants you to come, too. Can you?"

Vix's querying gaze momentarily shifted to Jay's. He gave a short nod.

She wouldn't meet anyone at Sherry's house who would talk about Jay's disassociation with her father, or who would mention Jay's Master's degree. The first was old news and the second expected and therefore not noteworthy enough to feature in conversation. He would tell her both himself before the job ended but not before, because he wanted her as long as he could have her. At this stage, every single day counted.

"Yes, I would love to," she said with a smile. "I can deliver the wine and snacks to them on Wednesday night, then."

"Maybe we could pick you up, too." Jay kept his tone casual. "I'll be Steve's designated driver because I don't drink."

She gave him a pleased smile.

Two hours later, Steve and Trent decided they liked the cheeses and the fruit, but Sherry would probably been keener on the pate and the little pastry snacks. Jay decided he was in love. The days without Vix had been filled with waiting and the nights had been lonely.

By pre-arrangement, she arrived at his house that night bearing yet more food. "It's my granny," she said, apologetically. "She thinks I might starve in the big city without Christmas leftovers and so you have to help me eat ham and turkey."

"When I get time." He picked her up, thoroughly kissed her, and took her to bed.

"Did you like my Christmas presents?" she asked some time later as she arranged the cold sliced meats on the plate.

She had bought him cushions in patterns of green and white, and a print of Monet's dark purple irises in a narrow dark blue frame.

"Yes, as long as the cushions are for you."

She sighed. "I know guys don't like cushions but these look so good in this room. I don't mind if they're for me. I loved your gift, which had better have been made specifically for me."

He had given her a big pink T-shirt to sleep in with *I distract Jay* printed on the front. "No one else. So, you had a nice time at home with your family?"

"The best. I hope you don't mind, but I told my father about you."

He froze. "What did you tell him?"

"That I'm helping you to redecorate your house and that two of his surplus red-gum shelves would look fantastic in your study. Plus, that you need them because the room is full of papers and books."

"And he said...?"

"He said sure. I told him about you all, and he thinks his precious baby daughter is in safe hands."

"Mine, specifically?" He couldn't breathe, his mind veering between hoping she hadn't mentioned his name, and hoping that if she did that James had kept Tim's funny business to himself.

"No, not yours. All of the construction team. I didn't single you out because…" She pressed her lips together and made a wide-eyed overdone scandalized face. "Daughters don't tell their fathers who they're sleeping with. I didn't want you to stand out because I didn't want him to think… anything. I'm such a prude and I have to work on that."

"Yup," he said, relaxing. "I'll help you. I know just the thing."

Chapter 13

Vix could hear the party from two streets away. Knowing she wouldn't drink enough to fail a Breathalyzer, she had decided to drive herself to Lex and Sherry's house on New Year's Eve. By prior arrangement, Jay would leave his motorbike at Steve's house, travel to the party with the guys, drive each home, and then ride off her house for the rest of the night so that they could spend the following public holiday together.

She circled the block a few times but finally had to park a couple of streets away, not too convenient when she had bags of food and a dozen wine bottles to deliver. For the first time in her life she blessed daylight saving. With heels far too high and a load far too heavy, she could see her way back to the right address. The heat of the day hadn't yet waned, and she knew her face would be red from the effort. She teetered through the rusty iron front gate. From there she took an unevenly paved path to the front door, which stood wide-open, blasting heavy rock music out into the open air.

Steve, dressed impeccably in clean jeans and crisp long-sleeved shirt, let her into the house. He bravely kissed her hot cheek, holding a beer bottle in his hand. Fortunately Jay, standing in the hall with at least five raucous friends, spotted her. He took her load and led the way to the kitchen.

"Hi, Sherry," she yelled as she entered the tiny old-fashioned room and Sherry looked up from her cut bread and fillings piled on central table.

"Jay, turn the music down!" Sherry smiled at Vix as Jay left.

Vix scooped a handful of cold tap water onto her face, blotting with a wad of kitchen paper. Her makeup didn't matter because the heat meant she wore nothing but mascara and lipstick. She unpacked her bags. The throb of the music faded slightly and now with less competition she said at a normal level, "I thought I would be one of the first here. Most New Year's Eve parties don't get this noisy until at least ten."

"Some of this crowd intends to party-hop and we happen to be the lucky first. Thanks for all the food. You've brought tons. Oh, and a cheese platter. That's a good idea. I've got sausage rolls sitting in the oven, but I don't think I'll heat them until much later, maybe after midnight. They're a bit unnecessary while it's so hot. It's so good to see you again. Did you see the boys' bedroom?"

Vix shook her head. "Not yet. I bought them Lego as a New Year's present."

"They love Lego. That's so sweet of you," Sherry said, her face plastered with a delighted smile. She wiped her hands on a tea towel. "Come and see the room and meet the boys before they go to sleep."

The room, a large but old addition to the back of the late '50s house, looked fresh and clean in Vix's citrus green. The older boys had a bunk arrangement and Oscar a side-less cot, each bed with a blue coverlet. Short blue curtains hung either side of the small window. Sherry had used industrial carpet tiles on the floor.

The older two looked up from the noisy game of trains they were currently pretending to play, using tracks inventively made out of quarter rounds nailed to either side of a strip of ply, Luke's handiwork no doubt. Various toys lay scattered around, waiting to trip up an unsuspecting visitor.

"Can we come out soon?" Max the biggest, another redhead, sounded disgruntled.

"When Uncle Kellen gets here, you can, but then, bed. Vix bought you a present."

Vix handed over the three parcels, assuming Oscar's would be snatched out of his puzzled grip as soon as she left. He gave her a wet kiss on order and the older two shook her hand, which she thought was cute.

By the time she got back to the kitchen, Sherry's sandwiches had disappeared, some of the hallway guests had left, and Jay was passing around cold bottles of beer.

"I have a carton of wine in my car and a lot more food," she said to him, taking her first real look at her beautiful, hunky man. As usual, he wore jeans, this time with a blue striped shirt. He had rolled up his sleeves, also as usual. The sight of his lean, hard, muscled forearms never failed to turn on her woman-meter. "Would you help me get it?" She wanted to hug him and kiss him, and stay in his arms for hours, but she couldn't in front of Sherry or anyone else for that matter.

"Where did you park your car?"

"A block over that way." She indicated the direction.

"C'mon." He scooped his arm around her and ushered her out of the front door. "That's going to be one big noisy party. How much wine did you say you brought?"

"Only a couple for the party and Luke's share of the Christmas hamper."

"He'll be pleased, but don't contribute any more alcohol to the party. The food you brought is more than enough." He stopped at the end of the street and kissed her. "You smell."

"Thanks."

"...delicious." He kissed her again, longer this time. His eyes shone darkly mysterious in the setting sun. "I love you."

"What?"

"You know I do. You couldn't fail to know. Now, where's this car of yours?"

Her face numb with shock, her chest thudding with joy and smidge of fear, she put her arms around him, kissed him shakily; then she guided him just a little farther to her car, knowing she ought to say she loved him, too. She couldn't, but she loved him so much that she ached. No woman could fail to love a man who treated her with such tenderness. Jay didn't see her as his possession or his efficient hostess. He saw her as a woman to cherish and protect. However, she needed a little more time and courage before she could say the special love-word to a man again.

"What are you doing next year?" She wished she hadn't asked and she knew that she probably hadn't asked before now because she was afraid of the answer.

"After tomorrow? First, I will finish the set." He rubbed the back of his neck, drawing a long breath before he spoke. "I'm waiting for news that I ought to get next week. I can decide then." Losing her gaze, he mangled the bottle carton open and loaded the rest of the food on top of the bottles. "What are you going to do?"

She shut the car door. "I don't know until the reviews come in for the show. If the set gets a review, I'm doing well. If it gets a good review, I'll be offered another job. I want a design job rather than a painting job, but I suppose I have to move up the ladder like everyone else."

"And I do, too. I need work experience, and I probably can't get any in South Australia." He held her gaze too long.

She frowned. "How could you possibly need work experience? You've worked for years and years."

"Not in the area I plan to specialize in."

"And what's that?" She squinted at him, momentarily blinded by the stark yellow gleam of the setting sun.

"The same as you. Design. Perhaps a bit of office work if I can get it. I want to branch out, again like you."

"Drafting?"

He nodded and hefted the carton up onto his shoulder.

The hovering sun cast a designer glow on the rooftop. She walked beside him, clinging to his other hand, plotting how to ask her father to find work for Jay in the area he wanted. Her father employed draftsmen. Without asking, she knew a self-sufficient man like Jay would hate being handed a job on a silver platter. Everything he had done, he had done for himself. He knew what he could do and he did it, unlike her. She kept trying until she succeeded.

But…she could keep Jay if she could get him what he wanted in South Australia. She could buy him, just as she had bought Tim. Her eyes filled with hot tears, which she blinked back. She didn't want her career bought for her any more than Jay would.

She had three guaranteed weeks with him, only. After that, he might have to move on to find the job he wanted. She knew without a doubt that he would never settle for less, but he was fantastic and any prospective employer would see that right away. All was not lost. The future would be left to the future and she would be with him until then.

She stared straight ahead to the house where people were celebrating the end of one year and the beginning of the next. The numbers had swollen in the time they'd been gone. Kellen came out with his two new dates, one on either side, and he took the carton from Jay. Vix followed to the kitchen and removed the food and started putting together plates of sushi, plates of nuts and fruits, cheeses. She was kissed by everyone and she laughed a lot. She had a glass of champagne. She talked to a good-looking young musician who wanted to take her to another party and she had another glass of champagne.

Her feet ached. Her heels were too high. One of Kellen's dates had latched onto Jay. Her body language said everything Vix didn't want to know. Jay fortunately said, "Nice doggie. Sit."

Vix wandered back to the kitchen, where she had spent most parties during her marriage. Her haven. She started to clear up. "Hello. We've met before," she heard a cool voice say. "You're JD's painter."

She turned. "Yes. We have met." She smiled at Lonny. "You're the friend who was going to help him paint his house."

Lonny looked stunning. Her long blond hair had been tastefully spliced with black, complementing her re-growth and making her winged dark eyebrows look exotic. She wore heavy purple eye shadow that cooled her brown eyes, and a loose top patterned in purple and gray. Her black pants clung to her long beautiful legs. Her heels were ankle-breaking height. "I hear you're doing a wonderful painting job yourself on his set. I've been invited to the last dress rehearsal, and so I'll be able to see for myself."

"Lovely," Vix said, trying to look thrilled that Jay had asked her. "Have you seen all the other shows Jay has worked on?"

"Most. I did the makeup for *Seussical the Musical*. That was Jay's first set job."

Sherry wandered into the room with an empty cheese platter. "The first set for all of them brought to them by—" She presented the platter theatrically. "Ta da! Ilona Liddell, stylist to the stars!"

Lonny—Ilona—clutched the platter like an award and smiled. Lonny looked like Tim's Ilona because she was Tim's Ilona. Vix had a sudden urge to laugh, which she suppressed. She knew she would sound hysterical. Her head whirled as she tried to put together Jay's few comments about Lonny.

"Best show I've ever seen," Lonny said, a pleased expression on her face. Sherry's comment had relaxed her. "Actually, it was the first musical I've ever seen." She put the platter on the table and began peeling prawns, which she dropped in a muddled heap in the center. Her long silver earrings, familiar earrings, one of which she had lost in Jay's two-seater, swung as she moved.

Vix had a vague moment of wondering if Lonny knew Vix had been Victoria Nolan. Tim had never called her Vix, and she hadn't called herself by her family nickname in all the time she had been married. And she didn't look the same. Her hair was now medium length, blond, and curly. During her marriage, she'd had long, straight, mousy-colored hair. She'd been makeup free—fresh-faced—as Tim had liked her to be, wearing tasteful colors like beige and beige.

Once, she'd been Ilona's antithesis and not long ago she'd been Ilona's clone, but now she was Vix. She doubted Ilona knew who Vix was, unlike Vix who for the first time in years knew exactly who she was, and who she wanted to be. Herself. And so for Lonny and everyone else in the world, she was nerdy, over-enthusiastic Vix, or Jay's painter, because Vix knew that unlike Tim, Jay wasn't with her because of her father's money. He didn't know she was her father's daughter.

"Would you like me to pour you a drink?" she asked the other woman, whose glass she couldn't see.

"I'm not drinking." Lonny glanced at her with a smug expression on her face.

"You ought to try this one." Sherry waved one of Vix's father's whites under Lonny's nose. "It's light and lovely."

Lonny stared at the label. "Maintree? Where did you get that?"

"Barossa, wasn't it, Vix?"

Vix cleared her throat. "A promotion. I'm a Barossa girl. I get lots of freebies."

"Tim used to drink Maintree all the time, but it can't be bought. The maker keeps his wines exclusive." Lonny stared directly at Vix, a crease between her perfect eyebrows.

"Yes. But he likes other people to taste them, as I said." Vix tried to look completely gormless, which wasn't as hard as she had hoped.

Lonny put her hand to the small of her back and rubbed. "I was given a dozen, but Jay and I drank the last a couple of months ago. It's a very good wine, but I'm not drinking now, thanks, Sherry. Health reasons."

"Liver disease?" Luke asked, clanking into the room with a handful of empty bottles, which he clattered into an empty beer carton.

"Very funny." Lonny gave a fake smile. "I think I'll circulate for a while." She left with the pastries.

"Have you ever known her to be that helpful?" Luke asked Sherry, planting his fists on his hips.

"Just an excuse to ooze up to Jay," she said flippantly. "Is it just me, or do you think he's a bit off her?"

"Dunno," he said, indicating Vix.

Vix gave a weary sigh. "It's hard being a princess. I miss all the best gossip. I might go and ooze up to Steve. He's looking quite dashing tonight."

"That'll be interesting." Luke grinned. "Steve could handle it, but I can't wait to see Lonny's reaction. She's been leading him around by the you-know-what for years."

So, Vix oozed up to Steve, who put a beefy arm around her shoulders and asked what she wanted, the outcome of which got his promise to modify the cupboard bought for the nursery scene in the musical, after which Lonny stopped trying to undo the buttons of Jay's shirt and hauled Steve off to another party.

Since this left Jay and Trent with Steve's car, Jay said he had a lift, thanks, and so Trent offered to drive Kellen and his two girls home, and a good partnering was had by all, presumably, including Vix, who not only ended up with Jay, as planned, but also might have out-bluffed Lonny. If not, she would do a Scarlett O'Hara and regroup: a good two-glasses-of-champagne plan.

* * * *

Jay had the best start to New Year's Day ever, lying on his back and being leisurely ridden by Vix, after which he lifted her off and sped up the pace.

After breakfast, they decided to do nothing related to home improvements. Instead, he walked hand in hand with her through the city parklands a street away from her house. After that, they window-shopped in O'Connell Street, buying a coffee before they meandered home. Home—her house, or his house, he didn't care.

"I don't know what you said to Lonny, but she seems to accept you now," he said, his fingers twined with hers as they entered by the back door.

"Didn't she accept me before?"

"She thought you were a bit too classy for me."

"So, either I'm less classy now, or you are more classy."

He laughed, glad not to have to defend Vix to Lonny any more. "I hope she's not stringing Steve along."

"I do, too. He's smitten, and he's such a nice guy."

The next day at work, Steve seemed not to think he'd been strung along and Trent was being cagey about the end of his evening. "Kell kept both the girls," Jay suggested to Trent, who wouldn't look him in the eye.

"Maybe."

"Jesus. You both ended up with them both."

Trent angled his head to the side. "Maybe," he said, his eyes narrowed.

"That's what I'll have to think if you won't say."

"Maybe is what I have to say or Kell won't share again, either one or both."

"You probably played bridge."

"Maybe." Trent shoved his hands into his pockets.

"Get the back out of that cupboard so that Steve can put in the seat."

"Where's Vix? I thought she wanted to paint Little Miss Muffet on this thing."

"She can't until you've taken the back out and added a seat and so she's gone shopping for the toys she'll have on the top. The cupboard's meant to show the scene is in a kid's nursery."

"Where else? I wouldn't have Little Miss Muffett on my cupboard—unless that was the name of one of Kell's girls." Trent snickered.

Jay left. His loyal workers had snatched back their independence, which suited him, bearing in mind that he wouldn't be around much longer. In three weeks, the set would be finished, and the schedule was tight. If the end loomed too soon, the guys would work overtime. Jay always delivered sets as planned.

Four days late, in the middle of the next week, he found the letter he'd been awaiting in his mailbox. Only an optimist would expect to win a nationwide architectural design competition, but he'd hoped his plan for a major Port Adelaide development would put him in with a bullet. He already knew he'd made the top five, but a win would give him a chance with Vix. His heart thudding and his fingers unsteady, he opened the envelope, skimming the wording and noting the check.

He'd won one hundred and fifty thousand dollars.

Light-headed, he walked into the house with the money, an almighty sum, which was the lesser prize. The real prize was that now he might be offered work experience with a South Australian group and possibly be outsourced to help build his design, that is, if the murk of his past didn't haunt him.

Expecting Vix any time soon, he left the check and the letter on the kitchen counter top, smoothing out the creases, rereading the wording, still dry-mouthed, unbelieving. When he heard his garage door open, he woke up to reality, snatched up the check and the letter, and shoved them back into the envelope. He had debts to pay before he could think about making a life with the woman he loved. At least now, he had a chance to be with her.

* * * *

Jay and his team worked steadily for another week finishing off the set. His checklist said each scene, sixteen in all, had every component needed, but he didn't doubt that the set designer would have a more detailed view than him, a mere carpenter/builder who worked to a set of plans. Any last minute adjustment could be made in the theater.

The next weekend, Vix finished off some of her extras at his house while he plodded along with his own kitchen cupboards. Now that he actually had a real future, he didn't see renovating his house as his only money earner and so he decided to enjoy the process as much as the end result.

Vix sat on the floor making her everlasting leaves—this lot, a set of painted fabric cut-outs with wired stems covered by green florist's tape—while he lay half inside a lower cupboard attaching hinges.

"We ought to take a coffee break soon," he said, his voice echoing back at him, and her phone rang somewhere in the house.

He sighed. She routinely lost her phone and now she would go on a hunt, tracing the call tune, which had to be the most irritating of them all, the William Tell overture.

"Where's my phone?"

"In your handbag."

"Where's my handbag?"

"In the bedroom by the sound of it."

She rose to her feet, clutching a handful of leaves, and hurried off. The galloping noise of the phone ended, followed by her voice saying nothing he could make out.

"That was Melissa, my stepmother," she said, suddenly appearing at the end of his upturned feet. "She and my father are in town. She wants me to drop everything and go to see her. She wouldn't say why." She opened her hand and let her collection of wired leaves drop to the floor. "That's everything dropped. I can't imagine why she wants to see me instantly and now I'm worried. It must be about my father because he won't be there." She picked up her leaves and placed them onto the countertop. "Do I look okay? I'll be back as soon as I can." She waited for a nod and then she pushed her feet back into her loafers, shoved her phone into her bag, and left.

Within minutes, the doorbell chimed. He rose to his feet and brushed wood shavings off his jeans as he walked along the passage, and he opened the door to a delivery driver dressed in a blue overall. "Shelves for you," the man said. "As ordered."

Jay shook his head. "Not by me."

"Red-gum shelves. From the Barossa."

"Oh, yes. Of course. I'll come out with you." He followed the man to the unmarked van and waited while the back doors were opened. Even from the street, he could see the gleaming red wood, the precise workmanship, and the value of the two sets of shelves large enough to fill one of his study walls. "I'd forgotten how perfect these are." He stepped into the truck and ran his hand over the wax finish of the nearest end. "Beautiful. These were made by artisans, people who understand real quality." Drawing a deep breath, he straightened, squaring his shoulders. "Unfortunately, I can't accept anything this valuable. I'll reimburse you for the full trip. Take them back, with my thanks."

The van shifted as another man he hadn't noticed climbed down from the high seat at the front. "And don't you appreciate real quality?" asked the man, appearing at the back doors of the truck. He wore soft tan leather shoes, cream chinos, and a red checked shirt. James Tremain, Vix's lanky, elegant father, stood foursquare, his fists planted on his hips.

Jay's jaw clamped. "You've been very generous, but I can't take another thing from you."

"Including my daughter?" James's lips barely moved but his light eyes flashed. "I suggest we discuss this inside. Roly, wait here."

Jay swung out of the van and indicated his open front door with one sweep of his arm. Without a word, Tremain led the way into the house, striding along the hallway and though into the sitting room. "Do you mind?" He indicated one newly upholstered art deco chair.

"Please," Jay said, waiting for the older man to sit before seating himself in the other. "And I do, of course, appreciate quality, which is why you are here. You're about to make me an offer for your daughter that you think I won't refuse." His jaw felt so stiff that he expected to hear a creak.

"You've accepted my money before." Tremain leaned back comfortably. His elbows rested on the arms of the chair and he meshed his fingers together across his upper chest.

"As I said, you've been generous. I mean to repay you."

Tremain made a sound of derision. "You wasted the opportunity I gave you, all for the sake of a female with the morals of an alley cat. Nice scar."

"Thanks. It has faded somewhat into this distinguishing mark. I presume the phone call was to get rid of Vix while you attempted to get rid of me."

"Bright lad, matriculated top of your school, top ten in the state. Not bad when only six altogether matriculated from your school, most of whom were your friends and now are your loyal sidekicks. You dragged them along in your wake. Was it worth the effort?"

"You know it was," Jay said in a low voice. "You would have done the same if you'd been brought up in our circumstances, but you happened to be born rich, which is why you try to compensate by offering the disadvantaged like me a leg-up. I'm sorry I wasted the opportunity you gave me, but there's not a snowball's chance I will accept any man beating up any woman, even if that man happened to be your so unworthy son-in-law."

Tremain dropped his gaze. "And so, to pay me back for supporting my son-in-law and believing his story, you've gathered my impressionable, vulnerable daughter under your accommodating roof. And you plan to make a good bargain before you set her free." He unfolded his arms, resting his elbows on the arms of the chair. "I wouldn't stop at the shelves, if I were you. They're worth upward of five thousand, and I know you wouldn't settle for that."

"Are you insane? I love Vix. Look at this room. She did this. From mixing the paint to covering the chairs, she helped me every step of the way. Add that to the start you gave me, and I owe you an enormous debt. Which, as I said, I will repay." Jay heaved a breath.

"After you get a job, I presume?"

"Right now. I have your own check for one hundred and fifty thousand dollars in my study."

Tremain's eyebrows lowered. "My check?"

"I won your design competition. Not, of course, under my own name. I didn't want to bias the results."

"You still don't suffer from a lack of confidence, do you? So, you plan to give me back my own money."

"Not all of it, no. Since you gave me thirty thousand a year for four years, I am proposing to pay back one hundred and twenty thousand and keep thirty thousand as my prize. It's not much in your world, but in mine, it's half my remaining mortgage." He stood, numb, his pride intact. Not so his heart. He would lose Vix, nothing was more certain. "I'll bank the check and send you your share as soon as the money clears."

"And so now we bargain for my daughter." Tremain stood, too, his eyes narrowed, his back ramrod stiff. "How do you think she will feel when she finds out you still have a dubious relationship with her husband's mistress? Yes." He nodded with emphasis. "I've had you investigated. How do you think she'll feel when she finds out you know she's my daughter? Betrayed, that's how she'll feel. She thinks she has befriended a new group of interesting people who like her for herself."

"She has."

"That won't fly. You misrepresented yourself. You're an ambitious young man with a lot of talent. Her first husband was the same. Like him, you think the most attractive thing about her is her money. I can tell you now you won't get a lot of it if you persuade her to marry you."

Jay wanted to indicate the front door, but he damn well wouldn't end this now. "I'm planning on earning a decent wage," he said crossing his arms across his chest.

James gave a brief, scathing hoot of laughter. "You'll earn sixty thousand per year at best for the next two years and to her, that's pocket money. That is, if you can get work experience in this state, and I can make sure you don't."

"I know." Jay maintained his stance, despite the ache in his chest. "But the set we're working on is hers, regardless of the designer and the construction team. Her painting is amazing, and I don't want to rock her boat before the triumph of her first night."

"She'll know you lied about knowing who she was by next week." Tremain raised his eyebrows in disdain. "We don't keep the name of our competition winner a secret. The publicity is part of the prize and gives the winner a good start, more often than not with Tremain's. We have an ad booked for the paper on Monday."

"If I hadn't told you, you would have used Jason Deene as the published winner. Why put my real name unless you want to hurt her?"

Tremain rubbed a finger along his bottom lip. "If I don't tell her a thing until after the first night, do I have your word you will let her go?"

"You won't take my word," Jay said through his teeth. "You didn't when I told you Tim hit Ilona. You didn't want bad publicity for him and so you threw me to the wolves. But for this win of mine, I would have been pretty well unemployable in this state because of that. I'm not now unless you go out of your way to make life difficult for me. That said, I don't owe you my word for anything." Shoulders stiff, he indicated the front door.

James Tremain tilted his eyebrows and left. Moments later, Jay heard the shelves delivered to the front porch and the van drive off.

Knowing he had to accept the gift for Vix's sake, Jay went into the garage and smacked nails out of old floorboards until he calmed down. Then he brought the shelves inside. His ability to see sense had returned before Vix came back, slightly puzzled.

"She only wanted to show me the dress she'd bought for my grandmother for the first night of the show. Well, she bought one for me, too, but I don't know if I'm going."

He hugged her too tightly, causing her to protest. A week. He only had one week more with her. "You'll want to be there on the first night. That's the night when you'll hear how much the audience likes the set."

"Yes, but what if they don't clap? I've often heard a set not clapped."

"They'll clap yours. It's light and bright like you and slightly quirky like you."

"Quirky? No one could be more conventional." She cupped his face and kissed him.

When she stopped, he drew a deep breath. "While you were away, the shelves for the study arrived."

"Oh, good. I had forgotten to give my father the address and he asked yesterday. How do they look?" A wide smile on her lovely face, she took his hand and led him into the study. "They're perfect for you. I'm so glad you have them."

Since the shelves were his payment for letting her go, he could barely manage a wry smile.

Chapter 14

Although Vix had met Jay a scant three months ago, she couldn't imagine not loving him forever. He was kind, smart, perceptive, and had a work ethic second to none, in and out of the bedroom. He was even-tempered, quick to laugh, slow to judge, and she couldn't find out what had happened between him and Steve. Neither man would explain.

Despite the fact that the two were currently terse with each other, the team had worked until almost midnight taking the set apart for transport to the theater tomorrow. Her job had almost finished. The set designer had seen and approved her minor alterations and Jay would direct the move. She could decide to be there or take a day off if she chose.

"I'll be there," she said to Jay, who for the past few days had been a little more off-hand with her than she would have liked—except in bed, where he was almost heart-breakingly tender. "But not early. What time do you think you'll be arriving at the theater?"

"We should be unloading by ten. Come after twelve and you can have lunch with us." After a too-quick kiss, he'd left at seven-thirty on his motorbike. Steve had decided to discontinue his pickups, which didn't appear to bother Jay in the least. He seemed to revel in the fraught atmosphere.

She went home, and as usual dressed in fresh working clothes for her day onstage, old jeans and a cotton shirt. After finding the designated parking area near the Festival Theater, she headed across a melting path of asphalt in the right direction, her tin of pencils, sharpeners, and rulers rattling in her big workbag as she walked. Her paints and brushes had been transported with the set, and she wished she had thought of a hat. The sun blared overhead, burning her neck. Sweat gathered on her face as she followed behind a trail of busy people, feet slapping, heads down, and not talking, to the backstage area.

Electric drills whirred, men's voices shouted over the noise, and someone seemed to be slamming wood against wood, repeatedly. Hesitant, not wanting to be knocked on the head by anything dropping, falling, or being carelessly swung, she stood in a backstage doorway, trying to spot a clear path through the sparsely lit area.

Parts of the set leaned against the black wall of the stage along with the new planks of wood that would be used to hold the components together. The Little Miss Muffet cupboard sat on a truck, the name for any transport that moved parts of the set onto the stage from the sides. Anything delivered from above, actors or sets, were "flown" from the fly area. At least three ladders of varying heights from sky-high to relatively safe had been set up. Black horizontal bars, tangled with electric cords and speckled with various globes, swung head-height on cables, waiting to hit the unwary. Apparently, the stage lighting still needed readjusting. Three men worked on this, while a woman called instructions from the control booth built in a cramped space above the front of the stage.

She heard, "Watch your head," from the woman, likely the lighting designer, and she froze, having learned from her work experience job to tread warily. The call hadn't been meant for her, apparently, and she didn't recognize anyone. Once a member of the team, she was now a mere bystander getting in the way. She cheered herself up by hoping something would go wrong that only she could fix.

A familiar head appeared from a trapdoor built in the center of the stage floor. Trent grinned at her, his face streaked with perspiration and dirt. "We're getting the pool organized because they're not finished with the lights up there yet. The lighting designer slept in and so now we're all late." He sounded cheerful. "Go to the green room. That's the first room at the back on the right. We put your leaves there to keep them safe. Lunch is in there, too. See you in five minutes." He disappeared and the trapdoor closed.

She found the green room, a cream-painted recreation area containing two long brown leather couches and a small battered kitchen. A new coffee machine sat on the counter top along with bottles of soft drinks in all shapes, sizes, and colors. Plates of sandwiches, stacked slices of iced chocolate cake, and muffins, all covered with plastic wrap, had been set up on a trestle along the far wall. Except for a bowl of assorted fruit, everything looked very unhealthy. She salivated, waiting for the others.

After a noisy lunch with the team, which now included a stage manager, a lighting engineer, a lighting designer, the theater manager, the production manager, various technicians in charge of the movements of trucks and flies, and the stage crew, she watched the other workers leave trickle by trickle to busy themselves elsewhere. Among so many people, few would have noticed the cool silence between Jay and Steve. Each spoke to everyone else.

Vix sat in the green room organizing her leaves into their various components. The wired greenery had a decorative role in the vases on the set. She would arrange these when the furnishings had been set out. The loose leaves would be attached to the background trees when the trees had been set up. While she automatically sorted, she speculated yet again about Steve's silent treatment of Jay.

Trent clearly knew what the problem was but he played dumb. Without bias, Vix doubted Jay had anything with which to berate himself. If he had, he would show signs of guilt, or he would try to make amends. Her knowledge of Jay put Steve in the wrong and refusing to apologize, which would explain Jay's noble silence. If this tension lingered, she would knock their wooden heads together, though not literally.

As the only person currently backstage, having finished the only task she could as yet, she decided to investigate and found the bathrooms and the dressing rooms, the latter already heaped with the costumes. The dressers, who were sorting various outfits onto racks, assuming for a moment she was one of them, were more friendly than the stage crew who thought, being a woman, that she wasn't. She stayed a while for a chat. Returning, she heard voices in the kitchen: Steve's and Trent's.

"No," Steve said, his voice grumpy. "Jay got her pregnant. He can look after her."

"She didn't say he got her pregnant."

"She wouldn't. And he won't say he didn't."

"Don't be a dick. The last thing you want is, oh…hi, Vix. How's it going?" Plastering a cheesy smile on his face, Trent left the room with the speed of light.

Steve stood, his big arms crossed, his expression pugnacious. "What did you hear?"

"What was I meant to hear?"

"Nothing."

"That's what I heard."

Steve left more slowly, after giving her a long suspicious stare. She sped back to the green room and sat, slumped, focusing on the worn carpet, not having to guess whom Steve thought Jay got pregnant. That would be the woman who currently wasn't drinking, who now wore loose tops. Dear Lonny. Dear troublemaking, man-stealing Lonny. Shaking all over, Vix lifted her gaze to the plain white wall, her mind whirling over and over events, words, scenes, and facial expressions.

Although not a good judge of men, she'd suspected her ex-husband, Tim, was having an affair. She hadn't fought for him because she didn't want him. She hadn't trusted Tim because she didn't love him. She loved Jay, and she doubted he'd ever tried to fool her. She doubted he'd ever lied to her although she recognized his evasions of truth, which pointed out his reluctance to lie. For example, she still didn't know if he'd been offered a full-time job although she had seen plenty of incoming mail from various companies, and she didn't know why he had received a letter from Tremain's, too. The opened envelope had been on his desk but had disappeared soon after she'd helped him rearrange the shelves on the day they'd been delivered.

For no reason she could imagine, except pride, Jay was now quite determined to let Steve suspect him of lying about his relationship with Lonny. A loose top didn't mean a single missed period. A loose top meant three or more missed periods—unless Lonny had decided to exaggerate her condition. Did Jay have a sexual relationship with her before he met Vix? He consistently said he didn't. Vix believed him, despite the silver earring in the depths of the couch, despite the key being kept by Lonny, and despite the other woman's attempts to imply a closer relationship with him.

Part of loving was trusting. Vix's mission was clear, and her place was beside Jay unless he could prove her to be a gullible fool. A man who could protect his younger brothers from their drunken father and teach a spoilt, untrusting woman the joys of sex and sharing with the right, generous man…

"Hi, there, Vix, sweetie." A beanpole with a shock of pink hair stood in the doorway. "I'm not here today. I'll be here tomorrow but everything is looking good."

She stood, smiling at the set designer she'd met in person six months ago but hadn't seen since. His sparse top hair had been blue then and he'd worn blue. Now he wore pink. Being outrageous suited Paul Evans, better known as Polly.

"I'm still stuck with the leaves, as you can see," she said, indicating the filled room.

"Poor lovey," Polly said without a scrap of sincerity. "I like your nursery wardrobe, and a couple of those lads building the set are simply delicious."

He sucked in a breath. "They're straight? Bad luck for me; good luck for you." He leaned over, kissed her on each cheek, and left.

Since Jay and Steve were acting like boneheads, she only told Trent he looked delicious.

* * * *

Until five that night, she wove leaves into a shaped greenery header the width of the stage and four feet long in some areas that would fly high at the front for the outdoor scenes. Without alterations to make on any of the flats yet, she had nothing else to do. The guys had finished the swimming pool and Trent had splashed Jay and Steve, neither of whom seemed even slightly amused.

"Jay," she said in an undertone, finding him onstage cabling the house flat to a fly at the back. "I'm heading home. Since you've got the bike, you may as well come to my house tonight."

His hands stilled, but he didn't turn to face her. "I'll be late and I want to make an early start in the morning. I think we should both have a good night's sleep."

"That sounds reasonable," she said to the back of his head, firming her jaw. "Especially when you're in such a deadly mood. See you tomorrow then." When she stalked off, she tried to look personally huffy instead of annoyed with whatever game he was playing with Steve.

She hardly slept at all that night. She tossed and turned, worrying about Jay, terrified that Lonny might have some sort of hold on him, until she decided she shouldn't be worried; he was a tough guy. Lonny couldn't force him to do anything he didn't want to do. Nor could she, for that matter, so then she started agonizing instead. If she didn't do or say exactly the right thing, she would lose Jay.

The next day the team finished building the set and a few actors began to wander over the stage, acclimatizing and getting in the way as she began to cover over screws, patch dents caused in the move from the warehouse, and paint two new uprights for the balustrade whose originals had inexplicably disappeared during the move. Oblivious to paint cans or other people, one actor took selfies in front of the parts of the set in which he would act, his scenery. The more experienced actors seemed to have a little more consideration for the set construction team.

Jay kept busy, organizing the working parts of the set, and she missed him. "Are you staying for the rehearsal tonight?" she asked in a voice she hoped didn't sound plaintive.

"I'll need to see how everything works." His gaze met hers for the first time that day.

A little breath caught in her chest. "I'll stay with you. I need to see everything in the proper lighting. I might have missed painting a screw or three."

He grinned. "We could cuddle in the back stalls."

Relief whooshed out of her lungs. She had almost begun to believe her own imaginings: that he planned to end their relationship soon. But he'd told her he loved her, and so he wouldn't leave her.

"Just don't mess with me while I'm working," she said, making her voice growly.

His expression softened and she could see in his eyes that he did love her. "I'll try not to. But you're mighty tempting."

That night in her bed, he held her as if he never wanted to let her go.

* * * *

On the morning of the last dress rehearsal, Vix called Steve before leaving home to make sure he was still planning to attend the show that evening. "If you're going to be the manager of the team after this, you'll probably—fingers crossed—be working with me again. I want to see the sorts of last minute changes that need to happen once the actors tangle with the set," she said in her most confident voice, "and I suspect you ought to as well." Her hands shook. Right or wrong, she would fight to the end for Jay. She doubted anyone else had in his whole life.

Steve took his time to answer. "Okay, since this is the last time I'm going to have to see a certain person. What time?"

"Six."

She and Jay would go separately, as usual. At exactly six o'clock, she joined the crew in the theater. The director, the lighting designer, the set designer, and the production manager sat in a row of their own, a black desk over the backs of the seat in front with a light trained on the script for the director, upon which he would scribble notes about every last thing he needed to address before the first night. During her work experience with a set designer, she'd had to stay back painting with him until four in the morning for one production because of the director's notes.

She acknowledged Trent, Luke, Kellen, and Jay as she sat beside Steve, a few rows in front of the executive team, hoping not to have to work into the night again for this show. She had expected Lonny, perhaps unrealistically, given the paternity speculation.

The theater lights dimmed, the curtain went up, and she saw her house-flat standing on the stage, looking spooky with the dark bay behind. Day dawned on the set and actors, some still in their own clothes, rushed on singing "High Society." Steve groaned. She patted his hand encouragingly.

Scenes faded and changed, and Steve stopped wriggling and sighing and forgot to dislike musicals. He listened to the words and the songs. He nudged her and gave a soundless clap as her nursery cupboard appeared and he laughed with everyone else when the youngest daughter of the house stepped out of her hiding place inside it. He concentrated deeply when the swimming pool arose and he leaned back with satisfaction when the surrounds looked theatrical rather than fake.

The cast took a costume break before Act Two, but since the same cast had done the same show in Melbourne for more than a year, nothing was expected to be a problem except for the blocking—the movement of the actors around the set—that so far had proved well rehearsed.

Grouped in the lobby for a stretch of legs, Steve and Jay ignored each other nicely, and out of nowhere Ilona appeared in tight red jeans and a flowing lilac top, her hair turbaned back with a wide patterned scarf. Like Moses parting the seas, she strolled through the dressers and wigmakers, the stage crew, and extraneous cast members to the momentarily silenced set-construction team.

"Sorry I'm late." She addressed her words to Jay.

He looked incredibly tense. "The second act will be starting any minute. We should go in."

"Hi, Lonny," Vix said, praying for Tremain poise while the other workers began to file back in. "I'm glad you could be here."

Lonny shifted her bored gaze over Steve; then, she glanced at Vix. "I wouldn't miss this for quids." She deliberately patted her belly. "I suppose you've heard my wonderful news."

"Not officially, but I think congratulations are in order. When's the baby due?" Vix held her breath.

"Six months."

"Tell her who the father is," Steve said in a mean voice.

"Now, who could he have been?" Lonny said, tapping her fingers on the side of her cheek. "Was it you, Steve? Trent? Kellen? Jay? Hands up. Who wants to confess?"

"That's enough," Jay said, clamping her around the waist. "We'll go in now."

"No takers? How very sad. I guess I'll have to bring up baby alone, then."

"You won't be alone," Jay said in a tight voice. He didn't look at Vix.

"Of course you won't be alone," Vix said, trying to sound sympathetic, although the three main participants in this melodrama didn't deserve points for anything other than sheer pigheadedness. "I don't suppose it matters who the father is as long as you have support."

"Of course it matters." Lonny planted her feet and stared mutinously at Vix.

"I'm sorry," Vix said, humbly. "I don't know anything about these things, but I can take one prospective father off your list. It's not Jay."

"Did he tell you that?" Lonny frowned at Vix.

The guys stood like statues, only moving their eyes.

"He doesn't need to. You're three months pregnant. I've barely let him out of my sight in that time and I've only let him out of bed to go to work."

Steve's jaw dropped. The other guys stared at Jay, who said, "That would be a gross exaggeration, and you don't need to take me off the list. I didn't mean for this to happen, Vix, and I'm sorry, but it's over between you and me. It was just one of those things."

"You cheat," she said, faking outrage. Steve and Trent flanked her. "That's one of the songs in the show, in the second act, as you know. If you plan to get rid of me, at least use your own words. As for who the father is, only Lonny knows, and you don't need to take the responsibility because she's not saying."

"I told the father of the baby, but he told me my baby could be anyone's. He would know." Lonny's chin wobbled.

"Well, then, he's a boneheaded moron," Vix said. "Let's go in and see the second act."

Lonny, her expression a sullen pout, turned to stare at her, but Vix took Steve by the arm and led him back into the theater. She thought she needed to give the baby's father time to regroup and see sense. Lonny sat at the far end of the row, beside Jay, her arms crossed under her pregnancy-enhanced breasts, her bottom lip jutted.

For a while, Steve appeared to be more interested in picking at his nails than watching the show. He fidgeted, sitting this way and that. When Vix sensed his body bunching to stand, she took a death grip on his arm and whispered her need for support. She almost heard the grit of his jaw.

Finally, the changing-hut scene began to play and for the first time, he sat still and silent, concentrating. Vix had made a mystery of this part when she had described the story. After he had watched the leading lady grow more intoxicated and less lucid, he muttered, "I don't know if she did or she didn't have one last...fling...before getting married."

"But you know who really loves her. Wait for the next scene."

He fidgeted. "Have you really been...with...Jay for three months?"

"Really."

"And you don't think he's been...with...Lonny in that time."

"Of course he hasn't."

"But you love him, so you trust him?"

"I couldn't love him if I didn't."

"And so if I don't trust Lonny, I don't love her?" He blew out a breath. He dragged in another. "But why didn't she tell me until she was three months? Why didn't she tell me right away? Because she doesn't love me. It's always been Jay."

"Shush. This is the wedding scene."

Steve watched in silence until the end and he grudgingly clapped for the cast, who rehearsed their order of appearance for applause a few times. "I do love her," he said into Vix's ear during the third run-through. He paused. "Always have. She always wanted Jay."

"You're going to have to explain all that to her, not to me. I've got my own problems. Jay loves me, but he's going to dump me out of misplaced loyalty to Lonny."

"Not if I can help it." Steve majestically rose to his feet and stared down to the end of the row at Lonny.

"I'm relying on you," she said, watching him crush the feet of every member of the team he passed on his way through to Lonny, who lifted her chin and began to leave in the other direction.

Now Vix had to deal with Jay, who had publicly repudiated her.

* * * *

The team filed quickly out of the theater, leaving Jay as alone as he deserved. He had lost Vix, as intended, but not the way he wanted, not in front of anyone. No one had spoken a word to him since, except Lonny. She had concentrated on Steve and how he supported Vix when Lonny was the wronged woman: "As if she is a precious flower and I'm only some old weed."

Jay now realized that Lonny had been trying to tell him about her pregnancy for some time. He didn't know what had held her back for so long. He could speculate, but he didn't really care. In pretending he might have been the father, he'd had the perfect excuse to break up with Vix, who had ended his little melodrama by discussing their affair. Openly. And by that, she had forced Steve to see reality for the first time in his pigheaded life, which left Jay floundering in a situation of his own making.

He'd known from the start that he couldn't have Vix, but he'd known she had him from the word "almost" in reference to her being a blonde. Add her father into the mix, and he couldn't get a job in Adelaide. Every one of his applications had come back with an excuse—no firm could offer him the work experience he needed to qualify as an architect. So, even if he could make himself redeemable in Vix's eyes, he couldn't support her. He couldn't expect her to live in the penury to which he was accustomed, especially when she'd never said she loved him.

He headed into the empty foyer, his jaw tight, his eyes unblinking.

Vix stood there, apparently waiting for him. "Do you think Steve's really the father of the baby?"

He shrugged and pushed his hands deep into his pockets. "It'd be risky telling him he was if he wasn't."

"Lonny doesn't seem to lack nerve. She was my ex-husband's long-time lady-friend, you know."

He nodded. "I know."

"And I'm James Tremain's daughter."

"I know."

"So, what was your plan for me?"

"I didn't know who you were at first, not until you smiled, and then I recognized you from a picture in the paper. I thought I would keep my hands off. I knew anything else would be dangerous for a boy from the wrong side of the tracks."

"I'm guessing here because I don't know, but I think my father arrived with the shelves."

He nodded.

Shaking her head, she heaved a sigh. "The scenario is really tired, but he doesn't know that. He's not a big reader of fiction—you know, the sort where the rich father warns the poor boy off by saying he'll disinherit his daughter."

"And he'll make sure the poor be-knighted lad doesn't get work ever again."

"That, too?" She clicked her tongue in reproof. "Should we discuss this over coffee at your house?"

"We'll end it here. I want work and I have been offered a single suitable job. That's in New South Wales. I'll be taking it."

"I don't want to leave my family and friends."

"So, it's fortunate that I didn't ask you to come with me." He took a step back.

"Do you imagine I would be destitute if my father cut off my income? I own a houseful of furniture and possibly a car. That's a lot for a woman my age. And I'll get another job even if this first one isn't appreciated. I won't know until I see the reviews after tomorrow, but I'm versatile, as I've been proving to you for three months. You can get a job anytime in building. My father has no—well, not a lot of influence there. And..." She lifted her hands like making a presentation. "You have a house, too."

"I don't own mine." He shook his head, his mouth tight. "To you this is a game—pretending to be poor. To me it's reality. I've worked all my life to get where I am, and I'm not giving up now. In the meantime, I don't intend to carry off a woman I can't afford. Not even if I love her."

She made a wriggly line of her lovely mouth; then, she let her gaze drop. "I have two tickets for the first night. You were right. I do need to see if the audience likes my work, just in case they love it. Could you escort me just this one last time? I would feel much more confident if you did."

He nodded. One last time. One. Last. Time.

Chapter 15

Vix peered closely into the mirror and made up her eyes to look wide and innocent, her lips softly sweet, and she added a touch of invincible pink to her cheeks. Anyone could apply clever makeup and anyone could be slim. Not quite anyone could put her father and Jay together in box at the theater and assume the night would have a perfect ending. She could—assume. She sighed.

Jay and her father had her best interests at heart, the idiots. Aside from the fact that neither had the right, neither should presume she couldn't look after herself. If she had to appear to be unable to look after herself to prove she could, she would.

She stepped into the dress Melissa had bought her. Melissa liked the family to be coordinated for publicity shots. Previous experience had taught James Tremain's second wife that some determined snapper would photograph him with his family on every possible occasion. Therefore, all the Tremain women would be wearing related shades on the color wheel, burgundy for Margaret, Shiraz for Melissa, and rosé for Vix. Being color-conscious herself, Vix didn't mind a bit.

Her only attempt at a dressy date with Jay had ended in her being inveigled onto his motorbike. Not willing to risk this again, wearing her truly lovely dress with floral shoes and bag, she picked up Jay in her car. He took her breath away, so tall and interesting looking with his tight expression and his scar. Tonight he sported a brand-new, grown-up haircut, short and slick, highlighting his incredible cheekbones. His slacks were gray and his jacket navy-blue. Her heart ached with love.

A card shown to the attendant in the booth entitled her to a good spot in the theater car park. Jay, like the perfect escort, opened her door and accompanied her into the lobby. He probably knew this theater better than she did, but he'd barely spoken. He had *good-bye* written all over his face. She hoped she had *I don't care* on her face but she probably had *oh, goody, a new play*, because she was better at being ready for a photo than faking a sophisticated withdrawal. Because her father had a private box, she didn't need to wait for the auditorium doors to open and she led Jay to the right door and up the stairs where champagne and a cold collation awaited. As did the adult members of her family.

"Darling," her grandmother said, kissing her on the cheek. She looked as beautiful as ever with her beautifully cut white hair shining in the light, and her makeup perfect.

"This is Jay Dee, everyone. Jay, this is my grandmother Margaret Tremain, my stepmother, Melissa, and you've met my father."

Her father took a step back, clearly astonished that she knew. "Dee," he said with a nod.

Melissa said in a delighted voice, "How lovely you could come, Jay," as if she knew Vix meant to bring him.

With her best little old lady smile, Margaret patted the seat next to hers, giving Jay no choice other than to sit there. Her father, not to be outdone, passed Jay a glass of champagne. Jay downed the lot in three gulps. Vix thought he might do an uncultured lout act and she saw a rough night ahead.

However, her father said, "Found a job yet, Dee?"

"I have a place with Barnaby and Symes in New South Wales."

"Do you know Jay, darling?" Melissa looked at her husband, nonplussed.

"I've known Jay for some years. He was one of our scholarship winners." Her father tilted his eyebrows at Melissa.

Vix breathed through her mouth. "He's an architect." She nodded as if she'd known. Design. Building. The letter from Tremain's. Her father must have denied him work...after giving him a scholarship? "He's brilliant."

Her father nodded curtly. "He won our design competition this year."

"Have a canapé, Jay." Margaret indicated the plate on the bar, which forced James to offer the snacks to Jay, who looked at the tiny treats with suspicion. He finally chose a goat's cheese and onion tart and looked pleasantly surprised, which Vix knew was an act. She'd presented them to him before and knew he liked them. "So, you're a fan of musical theater." Margaret stared at Jay with interest. She'd always been a terrible flirt.

"Not too much. Like Vix, I'm more interested in the sets."

"When I was younger, so was I, but we didn't talk about it so openly."

"Sets," James said heavily. "Not sex."

"Oh? He looks more like the sort of man who—"

"Mother," James said in a warning voice. "Though, likely you're right. He had some sort of ruckus with Tim over a woman. That's how he got the scar." He again stared a challenge at Vix, who was learning more about Jay with every sentence. "That's also how he lost his scholarship."

Jay stood, as if about to leave, and Margaret tugged at the hem of his jacket. He glanced at her face, sat back down, and folded his hands.

"I have no class," he said to her. "I didn't know how to treat a leading architect who was married to the boss's daughter."

"I'd say you did." Margaret covered his hands with one of hers. "If I had known what was going on, I would have done the same. Tim wouldn't have dared hit me."

"And so," James said, a bland expression on his face, "to pay me back for not listening to his story about the fight and taking away the scholarship, he bided his time, took up with Vix, and thought he'd get me to pay him off."

Vix's face froze. "So that's why he's taking a job at Barnaby and Symes. Normally you employ your scholarship students."

James cleared his throat. "Actually, before I had a chance to offer him a job, he paid me off, and with my own money, too."

"No mean feat," Vix said, needing time to compose herself. Her breath came in short, sharp bursts. "But tonight is supposed to be about me. The orchestra is tuning up and the overture will soon begin. Could we possibly take our places for the show?"

"Of course, darling." Melissa quickly finished her drink while the waiter cleared up. Like the patrons downstairs, the hirers of the boxes couldn't consume alcohol while watching the show.

Melissa shuffled the others into place, or tried. Margaret wanted Jay to sit by her and so Vix had to share him. She'd wanted him at the end of the row, not too close to her father, but perhaps that wasn't so important now that she knew they had a history. Although her father was as obstinate as Jay, she'd never heard him say a word to criticize Tim, who had grossly disappointed him, and he hadn't really said a word against Jay. He was merely filling in the gaps in Vix's knowledge.

"How did Tim give you the scar?" she whispered as the overture began. Her house-flat stood alone on the stage, surrounded by nocturnal semi-darkness.

"With his signet ring."

"I'm so sorry."

He shrugged.

"I'm sorry you lost your scholarship, too."

"It was time I took responsibility for myself."

She took his hand. He didn't resist.

The overture finished and the bay behind the house began to light up into a glimmering mass of water surrounded by trees. As daylight dawned on the set, the cheeky house with the geranium window boxes disappeared, the leaf canopy appeared at the front, the house servants strode on singing the theme tune, and the terrace balustrade raced onto the stage with the table set for breakfast. The perky cast kept the audience watching wide-eyed for a terrifyingly long moment but the effortless skill of the beginning soon brought a long round of hearty applause.

Vix sat, gripping Jay's hand. This was her moment, the set's moment, although she knew each scene would be applauded, not only for the cast but also for the wigmakers, the hairdressers, the costume designers, the backstage workers, the stage crew, and the construction team, though few audiences realized they clapped anyone but the cast. "They liked it," she said to Jay, grinning so widely that her face hurt.

"Casts usually measure up to a good set. They'll do you proud."

"And you."

"Us all."

She scrutinized each piece of the set as every new scene appeared, amazed that her imagination hadn't quite prepared her for the total effect with a magic, beautifully costumed cast giving their all. She came back into the real world at interval and turned to her father. "So, did you tell Jay that you would cut off my allowance if he married me?"

James took a moment to answer. He rubbed his chin. "I told him that if he married you, he wouldn't see much of it."

"Really?"

He nodded. "Uh-huh."

"And Jay paid you off. That means I have to live in New South Wales with him, I suppose."

"Did he ask you to go with him?"

"No, I didn't." Jay leaned back in his seat, watching her and her father.

"But you said you love me. You would want me with you."

"I can't take you away from your family."

"They would be thrilled."

"No, no," Margaret said piteously. "I would like to see my great-grandchildren before I die."

"I didn't ask her to marry me, either." Jay crossed his ankles.

Vix found a sanctimonious face. "My father would prefer me to live in a de-facto relationship rather than to have to pay off ex-husbands all the time."

Jay glanced at James, who shrugged. "Tim cost me a bundle. I had to pay out his contract. It would be cheaper if she went with you." His phone rang and he moved to the bar area to speak.

"Is that the babysitter?" Looking frazzled, Melissa arose and quickly left to be with him.

Margaret found a lace handkerchief in her handbag "I'm an old, old woman and my granddaughter is very precious to me. I need her here, by my side."

Vix prayed Act Two would begin soon. Her grandmother had a tendency to overact.

"Did you give my father your word that you wouldn't ask me to marry you?" she asked Jay.

"He knew I wouldn't take his word," her father said, managing to participate although he still held the unlit phone to his ear. "I didn't, you see, when he told me Tim hit his lady-friend. Take your seat, Melissa. That's the overture for Act Two."

Vix breathed a sigh of relief, although as yet the orchestra merely toyed with the tuning up. Her father had done all the right fatherly things like making sure Jay wasn't after her money and refusing to give him a son-in-law job. It was up to her to do the rest, and now that she knew most of the previous history, she could manage if Granny didn't help her too much.

The rest of the show flew by but she didn't really concentrate. She had a proud man to contend with, one who didn't know his own worth or that he had impressed her father from the very start, let alone her devious grandmother.

The show ended amid loud applause and after three well-rehearsed encores.

"I'm a success." Vix put on her jacket while Margaret dithered with her handbag, wondering aloud where her mythical house keys might be. She was staying in the townhouse with her son and daughter-in-law. "Now I don't need to worry about having my income stopped. I'll get more work for sure, Jay, even in New South Wales. We can sell my house and rent yours, or sell yours and rent mine, or sell both. And you'll be earning good money. I don't see a single reason for you not to ask me to marry you."

Margaret's handbag found a secure place under her arm.

Melissa stood totally still.

James paused in the act of taking the stairs.

"There is a single, very important reason," Jay said, looking remote.

"What?" Vix frowned. "Nothing is impossible when you love someone."

"Perhaps. But how do I know you love me? There's more to life than sets, though that's why you wanted me in the first place."

"Do you mean 'sets'?"

He cleared his throat, looking at Margaret, who was carefully not looking at him. "No."

Vix flung her arms around Jay, squeezing him tightly. "I love you. Of course I love you. I love you, love you, love you. And I love sets, too."

Margaret said, "Goodnight, you two. James, give him the job he earned. He doesn't want her money, though heaven knows why. Let's hope he changes his mind."

Vix smiled apologetically at Jay, pretending her grandmother hadn't mentioned money. Her father couldn't stop her income, which was why he had couched his words to Jay. Like Jay, he was the master of not lying and this had given her the hint that he might have been checking Jay out rather than warning him off.

Sometime, not too soon, she would explain to the most gorgeous, supportive, and generous man in the world about her inheritance.

* * * *

Six weeks later, Vix and Jay attended Steve's and Lonny's big white wedding in the enormous reception area of Lonny's favorite restaurant, just outside the city center. Lonny looked suitably chaste in a white lace designer gown and Steve was crammed into a dark suit. He now had the beginnings of a rock-star haircut, his biker shave growing with suspicious speed. Lonny had decided to update his look.

After dinner, the tables were cleared and a rock band took over. Each member of the band had a different hairstyle, each with dyed sections and shaved sections. Apparently, Lonny had made them a hit by deciding on their look. Stylist to the Stars, she was now calling herself.

Vix wished she could have merged into the crowd but she had come dressed for a wedding in an evening gown of pale yellow organza lined with silk, a very conventional outfit compared to all the others. In one way or another, most of the guests were famous, among them musicians, actors, television personalities, and even sports stars. Lonny's wedding would feature as the wedding of the year. If Tim had played his cards right, he would now be mixing with the sort of crowd he would impress instead of being a non-entity living in another state. Somehow, he seemed to have earned his just reward instead.

During the night, Vix enjoyed herself speaking to all sorts of people she wouldn't normally meet. Though, if she continued as a set designer, she would meet plenty of different and interesting people, as she was discovering lately. The Fringe Festival had begun and she had three small "gigs," the first as a painter of a couple of floats in the parade, and the next as the set designer and painter for a trio of opera singers.

"But for you, these two wouldn't be married." Jay curled his arm around her waist.

"The alternative would have been too hard to bear."

He raised his eyebrows.

She raised her chin. "Don't doubt it. I wouldn't ever have let her have you."

He whirled her into his version of a slow waltz. She didn't care that he hadn't been taught. He had natural style, either that or the sort of style she preferred. He simply held her and moved. "I love you," he whispered into her ear.

"And I love you."

"Two more weeks and then we'll be married, too. I think your father disapproves of our cohabitation."

"Are you marrying me to please your new boss?"

"Nope. I'm marrying you because I love you. I plan on spending the rest of my life with you."

She flung her arms around his neck. "That's good, because you're never going to get rid of me. And I'm not going to wear white, like Lonny."

The first time she had married, Vix had had a big white church wedding. Jay had left her to decide the type of wedding she would like when she married him. "Surprise me," he'd said. And so, she hadn't given him a single detail about their wedding.

He stopped moving his feet and kissed her. "Have you chosen your gown yet?"

"Yes. What do you think about scarlet?"

"The color?"

"Of course the color."

"Whatever you want."

She'd never had a chance to surprise anyone before, being so boringly conventional. The idea of surprising Jay on their wedding day had taken hold and she had found more enjoyment in hinting than she ever would have expected. He was as easy to tease as he was easy to please, the great big gorgeous hunk. She couldn't wait to see his expression when he saw her wedding outfit.

"It might be somewhat theatrical."

"Whatever you want."

Chapter 16

Whatever you want. Jay couldn't imagine why he'd said that. Since he had asked Vix to marry him after the first night of *High Society*, she had been holding secret meetings with her stepmother, her grandmother, and Sherry, whom she had asked to be her maid of honor. He had no idea what the ladies were planning but even if Vix decided on a themed wedding, he would go along with her. Her first wedding had been a travesty. Her second would be a marriage.

During the next two weeks, even the guys began to speculate. "What if you have to dress up like an actor in one of those musicals?" Steve asked, his expression ghoulish. For his own wedding, he had only been requested to wear the suit Lonny had chosen, and he admitted he had gotten off far more lightly than he had expected.

"I would love that," Sherry answered, laughing. As the maid of honor, she knew the theme—but nothing would make her drop a single hint, even when Luke had begged on Jay's behalf. "I can see her as the princess and you as the prince in *Once Upon a Mattress*, all dolled up in green tights and a nice wooden sword."

"Nice wooden sword. I'm not touching that one," Luke said, grinning evilly at Jay.

Sherry glared at her husband. "You know what I meant."

Kell ruffled Luke's red hair. "You'll need to keep your conversations above the navel, my lad. Ladies present," he said, indicating Sherry.

Sherry glowed with pleasure. Vix had made a difference to Jay's whole family, not that either of Jay's brothers normally had potty mouths, but none had perhaps given Sherry a chance to be treated like a grown-up, responsible woman. All three Dees had known her since she was fifteen and had never particularly treasured her as the wife and mother she had been since she was eighteen.

Now in regular conversations with classy Melissa Tremain and even classier Margaret Tremain, Sherry had developed a modicum of poise, and had even shortened some of her vowels. She was still as cute as a button, though. Luke had married well, despite Jay's original qualms about him being tied down so young.

"At least we have the venue sorted out," Jay said peaceably. "The great outdoors."

"Have you seen the place?" Kell glanced at him. "It's all very well to get married in a garden and I don't doubt Vix's father has a good one, but if it's too good, we won't have a shipload of fun."

"No, I haven't seen the place but I don't mind if you don't have fun at my wedding. You have too much fun, normally. I would like to see you with one date for a change, a nice respectable female who doesn't need to drag along a girlfriend for protection."

"I'm taking two to your wedding," Kell said, shoving his hands into his pockets and angling a challenge into his jaw. He was the best-looking Dee, a noir hero type, with dark hair and blue eyes. "One for Trent. Or, who would he ask? No one he could present in respectable company, that's for sure. I'm doing this for you. You don't want all your single mates turning up in the Tremains' garden with a crate of beer, ready to drink himself into a stupor to celebrate your loss of freedom."

"And you bringing a woman for Trent will guard us against that? You do realize, surely, that all my so-called mates have been invited, and that would be my brothers, a couple of lads from the university, Lonny and Steve, and Trent. None of you are likely to embarrass me."

"Except me," Kell said, his electric eyes flashing dangerously. "With two women."

Kell was still an enigma. He had said from an early age that he would never marry, but neither of Jay's brothers had been brought up in a two-parent household. Neither remembered their mother and both had been too young to recall anything other than the rages of their drunken father. How never deciding which woman he preferred to date would save him from falling for one was a mystery only he could explain. Safety in numbers, he had said.

"I am pleased and proud you have learned how to share," Jay said in a voice that could only belong to an older brother waiting for a swipe.

Kell duly obliged, though merely half-heartedly shouldering Jay a couple of steps. "What are we supposed to wear? Is it casual since it's in a garden?"

"If Vix is plotting some sort of theme, it will be for me, not for her guests." And her guests they were. Jay hadn't been expected to pay for a thing. Vix's grandmother had insisted on paying. She would also be paying for Jay's wedding outfit, which she said was her wedding gift. She also said that when she died, her two grandchildren inherited all her money anyway and Margaret may as well spend some the way she wanted beforehand. "I would suggest smart daywear, not jeans and a T-shirt."

"Do you think I don't know the difference between smart and comfortable?"

Jay grinned. His brother had a nighttime life Jay had ceased speculating about some years ago. Kell couldn't attract his night-clubbing women if he dressed badly. Neither of his brothers would shame Jay. Both were tall and good-looking and both were naturally courteous. Though, even the tough males from the Dee family would be overwhelmed, faced with Vix's wealthy connections. Jay sure was. He would have much preferred Vix to be anyone from nowhere, but she happened to be Vix and the only woman he wanted. He had to bear being married way out of his comfort zone because he wanted only her.

Her second marriage would be full of love and laugher and a ready-made extended family, all of which and whom she handled with style. As arranged, the day before she married she moved out of her own house to spend the night with her family in the Tremain mansion, where the ceremony would be performed.

In the early morning on the late March day of the wedding, a zippered suit bag and a large box was delivered to Jay's house, as expected. He showered and shaved and put off opening either package until just before he expected Luke, his best man, to arrive. After all the sly hints, Vix's first reference to *scarlet* backed up with her placing him in front of the TV one night and forcing him to sit through *Gone with the Wind*, he dreaded finding a velvet jacket in the suit bag, and a black cravat and a top hat in the box. The guys would rag him forevermore. Only for Vix he would stand tall and proud dressed as Rhett Butler, though the thought made him groan with pain.

Finally, the hour arrived and after stripping to his jocks, he drew a deep breath and opened the box, inside which he found another two boxes. The first held a pair of black shoes made from shiny soft leather, including the soles. The soles? Gray socks had been packed into one. The other held small red flowers on pins. He assumed he would wear one and Luke the other as a corsage. So far he saw nothing alarming. The shoes were pure quality and he wouldn't speculate about the cost. He had to get used to this sort of thing.

He could choose to be ultra-macho and insist his wife lived on his income but that wouldn't take into account hers, which would be a reasonable wage when she worked. It would also include her fixed income, which was anything but reasonable. One day, his would match hers, of that he was convinced.

For the past month, he had been working for her father in his massive office in the most junior position as a draftsman. From there, he would work his way up. This had been his dream for the past six years and, now achieved, still filled him with pride. He had earned his place by sheer hard work, not by romancing the boss's daughter, the beautiful woman he would marry in an hour or two. Steeling himself, he unzipped the suit bag. Gray. His breath whooshed out with relief.

Vix's grandmother had chosen a light woolen suit for him, a plain, beautifully cut gray masterpiece. She had added a crisp white shirt, which he instantly donned. He pulled on the trousers of the suit and searched around for the tie, which happened to be rolled in the pocket of the suit jacket. Placing it under his collar, he laughed. Scarlet. He would wear a red tie for his wedding. Likely Vix would be wearing a red dress. He examined himself in the mirror and thought he looked respectable.

His doorbell rang and he let in Luke, who strode ahead of him through the house. "Hey. The kitchen looks great. You've finished the whole thing. Those glass doors let in a heap of light. I might put them in my house."

"Once we had finished the garden, it seemed crazy not to put in the doors. It was Vix's idea."

"I thought you were going to sell the place."

"I'll put it on the market when we get back from our honeymoon."

"So, now you're having a honeymoon?" Luke planted his hands on his hips.

"The weekend in the Tremains' country house. They have a guesthouse there. The boss won't let me take any more time off than that, being a new employee and all."

"He's going to take it out on your hide."

"Yes. No son-in-law perks. Nice suit."

Luke glanced down at the dark gray suit he wore with a burgundy-striped tie. "I hired it. They tried to buy me one, but they can't buy all the Dees."

"They can't buy any of us," Jay said in a growl.

Luke laughed. "I told Vix I would probably never have another occasion to wear a suit and so she let me be. Do you reckon Kell will wear a suit today?"

"No idea. Here, pin this flower somewhere." Jay handed over the tiny red corsage and Luke didn't flinch as he attached the flower to his lapel.

He even pinned on Jay's without a word of cheek and then he escorted Jay out to his newly washed pickup.

"When I first met her, I never would have guessed she was related to the rich Tremains," Luke said, backing his car out of the driveway. "She wouldn't throw out that old paint. She sure doesn't spend the way a rich person does."

"I guess that's why rich people are rich. They make every cent count."

She'd made every cent count in his house, which she had finished renovating with his help on weekends. The place looked so good that Kell wanted to buy it but she wouldn't let Jay sell to him. "He doesn't need a value-added house like this one," she said in a severe voice. "He needs one he can add value to, so that he can make money and end up without a mortgage in no time. He's talented enough to do everything you did, and so he can."

Apparently she had the same plans for Sherry and Luke, who didn't appear to mind at all. Jay loved a very astute woman.

The trip to North Adelaide where James Tremain owned an enormous two-story mansion fronting the parklands seemed to take minutes. The traffic sped by while Jay concentrated on the crease of his trousers, rechecked the red flower, stretched his toes in his new shoes, and shot his cuffs, trying to listen to whatever Luke was saying. Vix wouldn't back out at the last minute, and yet, he still had a lingering doubt that he was good enough for her.

The doubt remained while he fidgeted from foot to foot standing beside Luke under a garden arbor heaped with white flowers. Water trickled from the vase of a Greek maiden who stood in the center of a fountain, distanced from him by a box hedge and a flower bed. Guests, possibly no more than thirty, sat on white chairs on the lawn and the sun shone mildly in the clear blue sky, the weather perfect for his wedding.

His gaze wandered to Vix's family, the women dressed in patterns of red, Melissa wearing red and white stripes and Margaret in red and white dots. Her brother wore a white shirt and gray trousers. The wedding photo would be perfectly coordinated and he huffed a laugh. He would have to expect his photo in the paper for the first, and hopefully last, time because of this wedding.

After probably a short wait, though to Jay the time stood still, Vix appeared with her father. Jay watched, transfixed as she walked slowly toward him. She wore a red and pink flowery dress and her unforgettable smile.

The ceremony lasted for seconds before she was finally his. The string quartet played "Who Wants to be a Millionaire?" "I do," he said for the second time, smiling into her eyes.

She slid her fingers to the crook of his elbow. "Cause all I want is you," she said, leaning into him, her lips curving with mischief.

"You know," he said during the wedding toasts, "I don't think it's such a good idea for us to continue the dopey tradition of naming our children in alphabetical order."

"I agree. I got to thinking about Quockadile and although it's a brilliant name for a boy, when he got to school, he'd be called Quockadile Dundee for sure. A better first name would be Che."

His glass missed his mouth. "I was never quite sure why I fell in love with you. I thought it was because you were smart and funny and sexy."

"And?"

"You are." Also, just plain wonderful. She'd made sure Steve married Lonny and to do that, she had to let the whole team know she was Jay's secret lover, not the sweet good girl they'd thought her. She'd made sure her family accepted Jay. She'd made sure of a job for him in South Australia without compromising his pride in the least. He couldn't see the attraction in bad girls when he married one so absolutely good. "What about Dan Dee? Or for a girl, Can Dee?"

His possibilities were limitless, now he'd found her.

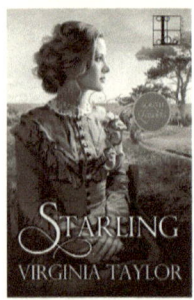

Chapter 1

Adelaide, South Australia, 1866

"Straighten your collar, girl," said the sharp-faced clerk guarding the office door. His olive jacket faded into the green-papered walls of the anteroom. "Mr. Seymour don't like to see his employees looking scruffy."

Starling Smith fingered the starched white cotton around her throat. She didn't look scruffy in the Seymour's Emporium uniform she had worn with pride for the past two weeks. She looked neat and anonymous in the plain gray. Any female lucky enough to be employed selling fabrics should be nothing less than tidy—and diligent, too.

Yesterday, when the owner, Mr. Alasdair Seymour, had toured the emporium he stopped to inspect the materials she had ranked using the rainbow color scale, a new idea of her own. He had taken her name from the department manager, and now he possibly meant to commend her.

His office door opened. "Miss Smith?"

Remembering her place, she leapt to her feet.

He glanced at his clerk. "I'm not to be disturbed. Come into my office, Miss Smith." Broad shouldered and tall, he looked younger than he had the day before, under thirty and handsome enough to deserve those sighs from the shopgirls.

Starling's knees wobbled as she hastened past him through the doorway.

"Take a seat," he said, taking his own. He wore his dark hair fashionably collar-length.

She perched on a carved chair upholstered in dark green brocade. The hovering red of sunset shone through the tall windows dressed with swags of yellow-striped silk. Sparkling motes floated to his desk where he sat, picked up a pen, and tapped the end on his blotter. His forehead was smooth, his nose precisely chiseled, and his jaw firm.

"Do you enjoy your job?" He looked straight at her. His eyes, an assessing luminous gray, sent a shimmer of panic through her.

She quickly lowered her gaze, trying to regain her breath. "I do." Her voice sounded embarrassingly husky. "I like working with fabrics."

"You worked in a hotel before you came here." He scrutinized a page lying on his desk. "They gave you no reference."

She had thrown away the crumpled piece of paper that described her as "a good worker," hoping she could gloss over the six weeks she had been employed at the Star Inn, mentioned in the South Australian police records as a site of gambling and prostitution. "I didn't think a temporary job would matter when I was waiting on the Seymour's list for more than a year."

He glanced up, his gaze again causing a strange jumble inside her. "You've had a small amount of education? That is, you can read and write?"

"Yes, sir. Or I wouldn't have applied here."

"Unfortunately, you've been annoying my customers." He set down his pen.

She drew a surprised breath. "I sell them what they want, sir."

"You sell them what you think they should have."

Shaking her head, she stared at her fingers knotted in her lap. "I sell them what they need. It wouldn't be right to sell fabrics not strong enough for their purpose or too heavy or the wrong color."

"And it seems you have decided on the colors they should have."

"I advise them on what might...suit."

"I don't pay you to advise my customers to buy cheaper fabrics than those they choose or less material. I pay you to make money for me."

"I do, sir." She leaned forward. "Just the other day, a young lady came back to buy more fabric. She said I'd given her just the right material for her ball gown, and she wanted me to help her again."

"Mr. Porter thinks the fabric department can cope without female staff."

"Female staff?" she queried, shaken. "But he told me I'm a quick learner."

He shrugged. "I'm sorry but I am not going to keep you at the emporium."

"You're going to get rid of me? Oh, no, you don't mean that. I get twice as many sales as Mr. Porter."

He shook his head, placing his pen in the holder. "I can, however, offer you a different position." He aligned his blotter with the edge of the desk. "In my home."

A quick shake of her head dealt with his offer of a maid's job. "I won't advise your customers about colors. I was wrong, and I'm sorry." Her voice rose with hope. "I would accept a position in any other of your departments."

"I don't have a position in any other department. I *do* have a list a mile long of women wanting to work in the emporium, as you know." He evaded her gaze.

Focusing on her weary black shoes, she exhaled her last hope. She'd loved measuring the soft fabrics, feeling the quality, and sliding the sharp scissors across the width. She'd loved working out the profits. She stood, not caring that her shoulders drooped.

He pushed out his chair and stood, facing her. "You could earn quite a bit of money if you accept my alternative. I'm much in need of a woman like you."

She straightened. *A woman like her?* "If you don't want me, I will get a job at Harris's."

"Unlikely, given that they don't employ females *with* or with*out* references. I won't beat around the bush." Pausing, he eased his black cravat with a forefinger. "You look respectable. I need a woman to pose as my wife for a couple of weeks."

Aghast, she took a step back. He didn't want a maid. He wanted to tup her. "I don't know what gave you the impression that I might do that, but—"

"Money." His lips tilted cynically. "Now, what would you say to five pounds for the two weeks?"

"No." Her jaw tense, she backed to the door. "I worked as a laundress at the inn. Not a prostitute."

He raised his eyebrows. "You only have to *pretend* to be my wife."

"I'm not good at pretending. I never have been." She opened the door and walked out.

Cheeks hot with humiliation, she strode past the clerk and down to the fabric department where, with shaking hands, she grabbed the cloth bag holding an apple, a clean pair of cuffs, a handkerchief, and a few pennies. Tying her shawl across her shoulders, she took the staff exit leading to a narrow alley off Rundle Street. She didn't have time to weep.

First, she would need to retrieve her belongings from the emporium's boardinghouse and next find accommodation for the night. The Star Inn might let her use the laundry room. If not, her friend Meg would find her a safe place.

Starling's chest hurt and her eyes prickled. As she pulled the heavy door, she noticed the purple haze hovering over the sunset. She stood staring, her dreams shattered and her life in pieces. Gathering her bag under her arm, she hurried down the cobbled alley, chased by the aroma of fresh horse manure and settling smoke. A hot wind whipped her hair across her face, forcing her to pause. Blinking hard, she tucked the strands behind her ears.

Dashing the back of her wrist over her eyes, she cornered into Rundle Street. Mr. Seymour stepped in front of her. His high-crowned hat cast a shadow across his features.

"This way." He seized her elbow.

She wrenched her arm out of his grip. "Let me be. I don't want your money or you."

"I have to have you tonight." He drew a deep breath. "I'll give you six pounds."

She backed away, disgusted. "I know at least three women who would accept your proposition. Go to the Star Inn and see which you would prefer."

He shook his head. "I wouldn't be standing here with you if I hadn't already tried that. None could pass as a lady."

"So, now you want a lady? I thought you said a wife."

"My wife would, of course, be a lady. I spent the last two weeks interviewing whores and actresses. Then I looked at my staff yesterday, and there you were with your careful speech, your background at the Star Inn, and your neat and plain appearance."

"Neat and plain." She firmed her lips.

"Good Lord, girl." His voice softened. "I'm offering you real money, far more than the fourteen shillings a week you earned here, to live a life of luxury for two weeks. You don't need to look at me as if I'm Satan. I'm giving you the greatest opportunity of your life."

"I had the greatest opportunity of my life—a job as a shopgirl." She blinked hard. "And for reasons of your own, you've taken my best chance from me."

His brow creased. "I'm offering you a better one."

"I have plans that don't include being anyone's wife, real or not."

"Two weeks, that's all I ask," he said in a long-suffering tone. With a sweep of his hand, he indicated she could move in the direction he wanted her to go.

She folded her arms.

He gave her a sideways glint. "I'll pay you *twenty* pounds."

"No." She wet her mouth.

"Perhaps you *won't* suit," he said, shrugging. "Mr. Porter said you were intelligent, but you are acting like a simpleton. I have offered you more than half a year's wages, and all you can do is persist in your belief that I want to bed you."

"Mr. Porter said I was intelligent?" Her voice rose with hope.

He raised his eyebrows.

"So, why can't you put me back in the fabric department?" She brushed down her sleeves, stalling while she thought. "I'm good at selling materials because I like selling materials."

He didn't want her as a maid, and he didn't want to tup her? She didn't understand what he wanted.

He heaved a monumental sigh. "And I'm sure you'll like pretending to be my wife because if you make a convincing job of it, I'll give you *forty pounds*."

Her mouth dried. Forty pounds! That was double twenty. For twenty pounds she could hire a little shop of her own. For forty pounds, she could not only buy stock, but also employ at least two other *Birds* from the orphanage. Robin and Nightingale would be her first choice.

Her breath fluttered. "You don't want to bed me?"

He looked her up and down. "Do you think you're my type?"

She put her hand to her hair and, blushing, quickly brought her arm down again. A gentleman who owned a number of emporiums, proving a head for business, wouldn't invest more than a few shillings in an untried, drab bed partner. He could take his pick of women.

"Well, what would the job entail *exactly*?"

"Just doing whatever wives do. Having breakfast with me in the morning, arranging flowers, eating cakes, drinking tea, sitting in the drawing room doing whatever you please until I tell you otherwise."

"What might 'otherwise' be?" She eyed him narrowly.

"Standing by my side and agreeing with every word I say while smiling pleasantly at my guests. You can smile, I suppose?"

"I'm not sure."

He gave her a suspicious glance.

"The job can't be as easy as you say." For forty pounds, there had to be a catch.

"It's as easy as you want to make it. I have a household that runs perfectly already."

"Then why do you want a wife? Other than to idle away the day."

Pushing aside his unbuttoned jacket, he slid his hands into the pockets of his biscuit-colored trousers. How he maintained a fit, broad-shouldered physique while sitting behind a desk all day was a mystery to Starling. Although she'd met no other rich men, she had assumed they were those with barrel bellies. "Last week my sister notified me she is bringing a lady with her, a lady she is sure I would like to see. She arrives from Victoria tomorrow."

"I don't understand."

"I don't like my sister's plan. She has tried this matchmaking before." His mouth tightened. "I told her I wouldn't marry any of her hopefuls."

"You don't need to marry the lady simply because your sister knows her."

"Nor do I need to have prospective brides presented to me so often that I give in out of sheer self-defense."

"Life is hard for rich men," she said sweetly.

"Exactly." He nodded for emphasis. "If I present you as a *fait accompli,* I will stop my sister in her tracks. So, are we agreed?"

She caught her bottom lip between her teeth.

"My deadline is today. I need to present a wife to my household by tonight. And, since I doubt you own suitable clothing," he said, averting his gaze, "we'll pick out a couple of gowns and, er, the trimmings before the emporium closes."

She deliberated. "I only have to smile, idle the day away, and agree with you?"

He nodded. "I want you to be as meek, quiet, and respectful as a good wife should be."

"And I will be a wife in name only?"

"That is our agreement."

Growing hope straightened her shoulders. Perhaps her dream was not lost.

He began to herd her along North Terrace. "I expect it will be worth forty pounds to prove my point," he muttered.

"That you won't ever marry? Are you a lady-man?"

His eyes widened momentarily. "A lady-man? Do you mean...? You do. Don't use gutter terms around my guests, or you'll be out of the house without a penny before you can sneeze. Of course I'm not bent. I simply want only one woman."

She could but wish. If she'd thought he only liked men, she could relax. "But isn't that a reason to marry?"

"I'm not sure intelligent and smart are the same thing. Enough. You have agreed to our bargain. The lady I want is already married, and it's time you became the sort of wife I require."

Starling nodded. He had specified a wife with a neat, plain appearance. She was neat and plain. Ordinary. Her body was slender, her skin was sallow, and she had brown hair and eyes. No male had ever glanced at her twice. At the inn, her plainness had been her best protection. Meg had told her she could be pretty if she tried, but she had no need to be pretty. She didn't want or need a man. In fact, her plan depended on her remaining single. No husband would let her follow through with her business idea. Married, she would blight more lives than her own.

She had nothing to lose by doing as he asked and had gained instead an opportunity to earn a great deal of money. She would obey Mr. Seymour's every edict. Opportunity had knocked, and Starling Smith only had to widen the door to reach her goal.

Half a pace behind Mr. Seymour, she passed the lawyer's offices, the pastry shop, the tailor, and a saddlery. The main commercial thoroughfare of Adelaide was familiar to her: the old wooden sheds, the new Georgian buildings, the constant grind of carriage wheels, the thump-thump of hooves, the bustle of people, and the push of their presence. Not only had she worked in the city, she'd lived nearby her whole nineteen years, watching the adornment of the newest constructions with ornate pillars and pretty plastered curlicues. She couldn't imagine living elsewhere.

Mr. Seymour pushed open the front door of his emporium. Dimly lit, the shop was preparing to close. He led the way to the ready-mades area upstairs and stood waiting for attention. The floor manager bowed from the waist.

"Miss Smith needs assistance," Mr. Seymour said.

The manager clicked his fingers for a shopgirl, who hastened forward. Starling knew Jinny, the red-haired assistant, from the boardinghouse.

"Three new gowns. Nothing gaudy. Help Miss Smith choose. I'll be back in half an hour." With that, Mr. Seymour strode away.

Jinny widened her eyes at Starling, who smiled and shrugged. Jinny moistened her lips and bustled about finding ready-made gowns while Starling stood by her left shoulder, pointing out those she wanted. Brown, being the cheapest dye, had been the color for the foundlings. She had worn brown her whole life until two weeks ago, when she'd exchanged that color for the gray of the Seymour uniform. Knowing neither flattered her, she decided that because this handsome man had chosen a plain woman for his bride, she should not try to change her appearance.

She kept on the last gown she tried. Patterned in a jaundiced green and brown, the high-buttoned fit was as unflattering as the other two she'd chosen. Continuing her disapproving silence, Jinny parceled them and Starling's uniform. When Mr. Seymour returned, he took the purchases, cramming them with a few other parcels into a new holdall. Next, he let Starling choose a plain brown hat. She wore that, too, certain she looked even more thin faced wearing a flat-brimmed poke with a long ribbon tie.

Finally, he took her to the jeweler's shop and bought her a plain gold ring. Keeping her face expressionless, she slid on the circlet. How she would pass as the wife of a gentleman, she didn't know. Nor did she know why he thought she might. She could only hope that the colors she had chosen to wear would merge her into the background, as she didn't plan to lose the forty pounds before she'd seen a single penny.

When he marched her outside the shop again, she totaled his purchases: one pound for the ring and more good money for a hat and gowns. He had shelled out a tidy sum to deceive a sister who merely wanted to see him happily married. Starling hoped she could play her unworthy role.

She kept pace with him, her bonnet ribbons fluttering as she moved closer to her goal. Eagles might soar. Starlings took chances when they saw them.

Meet the Author

From art student to stylist, to nurse and midwife, **Virginia Taylor's** life has been one illogical step to the next, each one leading to the final goal of being an author. When she can tear herself away from the computer and the waiting blank page, she immerses herself in arts and crafts, gardening, or, of course, cooking. You can visit her website at www.virginia-taylor. com, and tweet her @authorvtaylor.